THE STRICTLY BUSINESS PROPOSAL

Freshwater Bay Series

Nell Grey

CONTENTS

ABOUT NELL GREY

Sign up to Nell Grey's newsletter for news about Nell Grey's novels, plus access to some great book offers.
https://mailchi.mp/4ef191200d94/nell-grey

Books By Nell Grey

The Freshwater Bay Series:
The Strictly Business Proposal - Gareth and Beth
The Actor's Deceit - Rhys and Ariana
Their Just Deserts - Owen and Alys
The Rural Escape - Madog and Jo

Trust Me Find Me Series
Trust Me
Find Me

A SPELLBINDING DRAMA THAT WILL HAVE YOU ENTHRALLED
★ ★ ★ ★ ★
"I was so entranced by the story that I read it in one sitting,
I couldn't put it down!"
"An absolute page turner"
"Beautifully written"

CHAPTER 1

---------✳---------

L a Vie en Rose was bouncing again. It was standing room only on the sunny riverside terrace and all the tables of this swanky London restaurant were booked out.

A few metres away in the restaurant's hot kitchen, Chef Barnes was busting a gut to get the orders out on time.

Five foot two and slight, many underestimated her at first. But boy, did they make a mistake if they did. Because Beth Barnes controlled La Vie's kitchen like a military commander. And right now she could see she had a man down.

Her newest recruit on the fish station was about to lose it. His face was beetroot-red, his workstation a war zone. She'd already sent back two dishes for him to re-plate.

She called over to him.

"How much longer on table five's scallops?"

"Two minutes, Chef... *Argh!*"

The pan slid through his fingers but landed back on the hob.

She went over and patted his arm.

"Alright, calm down. I'll plate this one."

She took the caramelised scallops over to a dish she'd put out on the bench.

"You're doing fine. They're cooked perfectly, you just need to work on your presentation."

He stared at her uncertainly.

"Yes, Chef."

She began spooning a shiny oval of herbed mousse onto the plate.

"When you do a quenelle I want it like this, see? Smooth like an egg."

She took the dish over to the pass, where three other plates sat waiting for her approval.

"Service, please! Starters to table five. Quick as you can."

A waiter whisked them away.

Beth turned back to the new recruit and the scallops on the stove.

"Go cool off and I'll get the rest of these checks out."

She shucked another pan then looked the new chef in the eye.

"I want you back here in five minutes to clear this mess up, alright?"

"Yes, Chef."

Another check. Beth stretched out her hand to the waiter.

"One goat's cheese, four turbot," she called out.

Two chefs de partie sprang into action.

"Oui, Chef."

"Oui, Chef."

Beth's own creation, the lunchtime special of turbot with a Pernod velouté sauce was flying out. Marcel, her French boss would be popping a champagne cork when he counted up the takings.

Still, she couldn't help but feel worried.

She glanced at her watch again.

Evan Morgan came in every Friday at two. Table twelve. It was his thing. And this was the second Friday he hadn't turned up.

He hadn't cancelled and he was now well over two hours late. It was so not like him.

"Is table twelve still a no show?"

The waiter, a cocky university student, checked the booking system for her again.

"What is it with you and that old dude anyways? You gotta thing for older men, Chef?"

She gave him a withering stare.

"I'm ready to plate table twenty. Go clear their starters."

She shrugged as the waiter sloped off.

What was wrong with hanging out with Evan? They were both alone in London. He was a retired chef; a food geek like her. Plus, she loved his scandalous stories from the Paris and London kitchens he'd worked in. He was full of it, alright.

And when they'd had a couple of glasses of wine he'd tell her about Monique, his French wife, and his restaurant back in Wales by the sea.

It sounded magical. When Monique died, his heart died too, he'd told Beth. Not being able to face being there without her, he'd come back to London. Back to the company of chefs.

And anyway, Evan was her mentor.

When she was bouncing her recipe ideas around, Evan would always be there, chipping in with suggestions. Flavour combinations, techniques, textures.

Evan was old school. Classical French. He told her quite candidly he'd happily live out the rest of his days without eating quinoa or tofu ever again. And some of the new cooking methods totally befuddled him.

"You're doing Frankenstein food again, my dear," he joked when she told him how she'd been using liquid nitrogen to set her green apple sorbet.

That said, he did adore tasting Beth's creations.

She sighed.

He'd helped her think up that turbot dish.

"You've nailed it," he'd told her as he tried it. "Of course, the secret's in that Pernod sauce of yours."

That had been his idea.

Perhaps Evan had a bug and had forgotten to cancel?

She really had meant to call him but she'd been busy covering shifts. Then, somehow the week had zipped by and it had totally slipped her mind. Until now.

"OK, that's us done."

Beth wrapped up her lunchtime team.

"Great job, guys. We've got a very full box of tips today."

She mouthed good luck to Gary, the other managing chef, who was taking the evening shift.

Gary's eyes raked over her for a moment too long. He'd been hinting for a while now about them getting together. He was a good-looking guy, but no way was she going there. She knew to her cost that dating co-workers was a dumb idea.

She brushed past him and went to find her friend Alys who was heading up the pastry section.

"I'm gonna go to Evan's place later, " she told Alys. "Check he's alright."

Alys passed Beth a loaf of her freshly-made sourdough bread.

"Give him this. And take some of that pea and wild garlic soup too."

Beth wrapped the bread in clingfilm. Just smelling it was enough to put two dress sizes on her.

Alys handed her the soup in a plastic box.

"And ask him to call me. I want that pain couronne recipe he was telling me about."

With the plastic box of soup and the loaf in one hand, Beth stood outside her house and fished in her bag for her keys.

Still juggling, she unlocked the door and picked up the post off the hall floor. She flicked through the envelopes and put all but one onto the side table for the other tenants.

The stiff envelope in her hand was addressed to her.

Please let it not be another wedding invitation, she muttered to herself out loud.

She hated weddings.

Friends settling down, having kids. Making her feel single and lonely when most of the time she was perfectly happy with her life. Her busy career. The freedom to do what she wanted, whenever she wanted.

She put her finger under the sealed edge, tearing it open. Whoever this was from, she'd politely decline.

She was right. It was an invitation.

But this was different.

There was a formal black edging around it, and it was hand-written.

'Dear Miss Beth Barnes,

We regret to inform you that your friend Mr Evan Morgan passed away peacefully on March 3rd.

You are invited to attend his funeral at Freshwater Bay Chapel, 12pm March 19th, followed by a meeting with ourselves at 2pm in Le Gallois Restaurant, Freshwater Bay.

We look forward to meeting with you and extend our profound sorrow for your loss.'

Mr David Davies, Solicitors.

Evan was dead.

She read it again.

Had he died in his sleep? Had he been ill?

Oh no! And she hadn't called him.

She did the maths in her head. He must have died over two weeks ago.

She swallowed a hard, painful lump in her throat as the guilt and questions swimming through her mind made her feel dizzy.

Had they found him dead? Had he been alone in his flat? What if he'd been taken ill and died before he could reach the phone?

The box of soup slipped from her fingers and splattered across the tiled hallway floor.

Shit!

She wiped her wet face with the back of her hand and went to find a mop.

March 19th. Monday. It was Friday now.

How on earth was she going to get off work and all the way to the west of Wales in two days' time?

Saturday evening, Beth sank into her sofa and sipped a glass of La Clape Languedoc red wine, a bottle she'd been saving.

"To Evan," she toasted skywards.

She hoped he was with Monique.

As predicted, Marcel had been in an extremely good mood following the busy Friday service.

"Take a few days off," he told her. "Of course, you must go."

Beth felt bad. It was such short notice.

"If you need me back, call me, okay?"

"But it's far, is it not?"

"About five hours. Probably six in my clapped-out car."

The End of the World Evan called it, right at the tip of the West Wales peninsula.

She'd booked three nights at the Lobster Pot Inn, Freshwater Bay's only pub. The online reviews weren't great but it was cheap.

"Beth, forget about work. Take a break," Marcel had told her.

She sighed. She couldn't remember when she'd last taken a holiday.

Evan was always going on about Freshwater Bay. Was it bad that she was looking forward to going?

Beth closed her eyes. She imagined herself sitting on the beach. Her toes buried deep in the soft sand. Her face and shoulders warmed by the sun. And as she dreamed, she conjured up a delicious dish of grilled mackerel with a rich tapenade dressing. She definitely needed to make that.

And she might even get to meet Evan's family while she was there. He was still close to his brother and his wife.

Evan loved a good gossip about them. Especially his four nephews. She felt like she knew them already.

The eldest had only gone and found his girlfriend bonking his best mate. Skipped the gym after work and walked in on them, at it in their bedroom.

"Hell of a good lad, Gareth. An architect," Evan had winked at her. "Great vision. Totally blind about *her*, mind. He wanted to do some business with me a while back. But I thought best not to... not until he's free of that floozy."

The second nephew was a rugby player. He sent Evan tickets. The third, apparently, was a Hollywood actor. Beth had never heard of him. And the youngest, Madog was home on the farm.

Evan had been terribly cut up a few months back. Madog's girl-friend had died giving birth. She was twenty-four. Madog was bringing up the baby as a single dad.

The Morgans certainly had their fair share of troubles. But still, it must be nice to be part of a large family, Beth thought. Not that she'd know. It had always been just her and her mum. And now it was just her.

Evan was like the granddad she wished she'd had. And with no kids of his own, Evan had taken to her too. He listened patiently when she offloaded about work and what she'd been up to with her friends.

On their last meeting, she'd been telling him about Dave and her disastrous date.

She'd got to how he'd been taken off in the police van when Evan erupted with laughter, making her giggle too.

"Stop it. It's not funny."

Evan wiped his wet eye with his cotton handkerchief.

"Beth, why do you always seem to pick 'em?"

He dipped his shortbread into his latte.

"Forget this online dating rubbish."

He made for his pocket. His blue eyes sparkled at her.

"I'm sure I can find you a nice young man. I've a few in here."

She stretched her hand across, touching his arm.

"Thanks, but no thanks."

Evan continued scrolling through his phone contacts regard-less, rubbing it in.

"Well, you need some serious help, my girl. What did I call that last one, again? The one you went out with before this Disastrous Dave?"

"Luke the Leak."

"Ah, yes. The plumber."

She rolled her eyes and drained her espresso. He'd fixed her tap and flooded the flat below.

Evan chuckled, remembering too.

"Beth, how can you have such great taste in food and such bad taste in men?"

Beth sighed sadly. She'd even told Evan about Jean-Paul. The chef who'd broken her heart and sent her running home from Paris nine years before.

They'd never talk together again.

Twenty-nine years old, lonely and a little bit drunk, Beth suddenly felt an urge within her.

She needed to do more with her life.

What exactly it was she needed to do, she didn't know. But she promised herself she'd figure it out soon.

By Sunday morning, though, she was still none the wiser. And that same feeling of dissatisfaction still lingered inside her.

She badly needed a break.

With some banging beats in her ears, Beth Barnes headed out of London in her little car.

Taking the motorway west, the city gradually gave way to fields and she could feel her mood lifting. She was not sure why when she was going to a funeral, but this trip was starting to feel like a new beginning.

CHAPTER 2

----------*---------

I t was well into the afternoon when Gareth Morgan peered up from his sander in the old boathouse he was renovating and was caught again by the stunning beauty of the sea.

Bright sunlight streaked across the bay turning the grey waters silver. The sea was dead flat calm and there was warmth in the spring air after the long, wet winter.

He put his tools down.

It was Sunday after all. He'd earned himself a paddle.

He loaded his kayaking gear into the pickup truck and took off up the steep track from the boathouse past his uncle's old restaurant on the clifftops.

He paused when he reached the empty car park. It was so quiet here now compared to when the restaurant was in full swing.

For some reason, Uncle Evan had never sold the place. His dad told him quietly that Evan had been offered a couple of million by a developer for the land and restaurant, but he'd declined it. He said they'd ruin the place and it would never be like it was again.

After he'd split with Chantelle, Gareth had written to his uncle with his plans. He wanted to keep it formal; it was a business proposal after all, and he didn't want his uncle to feel obligated.

He'd suggested a lease agreement to secure the fields opposite the restaurant for a development of eco-chalets. He planned five high-end luxury holiday rentals alongside five homes for locals.

He may be a humble builder now, but his designs were the latest in zero-impact builds, using cutting edge materials and techniques.

He'd hoped this development would enhance the community. Property prices were sky-high. Any house that came on the market was instantly snapped up by online buyers wanting holiday homes.

The village was changing and there was talk that the school might have to close. Jake, his new baby nephew, would have to travel ten miles to the nearest school every day.

He'd had no reply from his uncle about the development. He presumed it was a no. Well, it certainly was now. The solicitor's meeting after the funeral tomorrow would confirm that.

The land would inevitably be sold and developed by some multi-million-pound company, building more characterless condos for summer weekenders.

From the restaurant, the peninsula of cliffs stretched out to sea like a finger pointing at the uninhabited islands that peppered the bay in front of him. The flat fields on the cliff tops swept back inland, back to the mountains that kept Freshwater Bay sheltered from the cold easterly winds.

It was a damn fine view.

And it was the best damn thing he ever did that spur of the moment day when he resigned. When he'd traded his brand new VW Golf for a pickup truck, bought some tools and headed back west.

Underneath everything, there had always been the longing to be back home.

The hard truth was that his marriage had been over for a long while before that fated evening. That total cliché. Two bodies wrapped together. Naked, on his bed.

His bruised ego had healed and his heart had hardened. By now, he felt only regret. Regret for marrying her in the first place. Once he could coolly reflect on it, the divorce was a huge relief.

He started the pickup's engine and drove down the hill from the old restaurant to the harbour front. Then, in his kayak he slipped into the silvery sea.

He paddled past the jetty where he was currently camped in his dad's sailboat.

Living on the boat was cramped, but it did help him focus on getting the boathouse finished.

Going back home hadn't been an option. He'd gotten used to his own space and he liked it that way. With Jake to care for and the farm, they were all busy enough without him around.

Gareth paddled around the bay in his kayak for a while before heading towards the boathouse.

It had been a fair wreck when his dad gave it to him. A large, wooden shed that had been in the family for generations. It was set on the rocks safe from the winter storm waves with a rickety deck and a slipway down to the sea.

And now, the boathouse would be his first eco-home. It was still pretty much a shell inside and he had to live on the boat for now, but at least he'd made the outer structure sound. And it stood newly painted, abutting the sea.

It was almost sunset when Gareth finished paddling. He pulled his kayak up alongside the harbour jetty.

As with every Sunday evening, after the weekenders had gone home Freshwater Bay was wonderfully tranquil. It was his favourite time there.

No one was about except for a young woman who was getting out of a small beat-up hatchback in the pub car park.

It was her hair that first drew his attention. The lowering sun shone on the long waves of her blonde tresses turning them into thousands of strands of glistening gold.

Then, he noticed how her v-necked green sweater clung snuggly around the curves of her breasts and her small, delicate body. And how her tight jeans stretched around a delicious butt and a pair of slender legs.

She was on her phone walking towards the harbour front.

He turned away.

But after a couple of seconds, he couldn't help himself. He sneaked another peek as she strolled casually away from the harbour and into The Lobster Pot Inn, carrying a small suitcase.

She was petite and blonde. Not his usual type at all. Yet, there was something about her. He couldn't keep his eyes off her.

He checked himself. He needed to get out more. He'd been spending way too much time sanding floorboards.

When was he last in The Lobster Pot? A couple of weeks ago? More? He'd put himself out of the game.

He promised himself to go down to Cardiff to see Owen soon. His rugby star brother had women dripping all over him. They'd go to a club. Find some hot girls who were up for some fun. No relationship crap, no betrayals. *Man*, he needed to do something.

As hot girls went though, this one would fit the bill nicely. Horny tourists were part of the perks of living in Freshwater Bay. He'd swing by The Lobster Pot later, try and casually bump into her.

Ariana would know who she was. She worked there. She knew everything that was going on. He could talk to her about anything, except his brother Rhys.

That was fine by him. He wasn't sure why they'd split up; he'd been away at university at the time. But his brother had been a dick, especially after he started hanging out with his druggie buddies.

Hot Shot wasn't coming home for Uncle Evan's funeral. Mam was always defending him. But Rhys hadn't been home in five years and he rarely called them. Apparently, he was filming in New York. He'd sent Mam and Dad a condolence card, which was big of him.

At last, she was there. In Freshwater Bay. After a slow, torturous journey in her little car, Beth was exhausted.

"Just arrived," she told Alys on the phone. "And it's exactly how Evan described it. It's so peaceful here. There are boats in the harbour and this really pretty row of white cottages. And the pub I'm staying in, it's a bit scruffy, but it's in a fabulous location. It's across the road from the harbour."

She paused and took in a tall, dark-haired canoeist pulling himself out of his kayak onto the jetty.

"It's *quite* a view."

She was trying not to check him out, she really was. But she couldn't help but notice how his shoulder muscles flexed under his tight grey t-shirt as he lifted himself out of the water.

A girl needed something to think about through the long, lonely night that awaited her. And he'd do just fine.

The reviews were spot on. The Lobster Pot Inn had seen better days. But despite the outdated decor and the sticky carpet, it had a homely feel.

Beth walked up to the empty bar, and a tall, Italian-looking woman quickly appeared from the back office.

She gave Beth a broad smile as she noticed the suitcase.

"Hi there. Are you checking in?"

"Yes. Beth Barnes. I've booked online for the four nights."

She flicked through the big desk diary.

"Yep, I've got you right here."

"Wow! I love those."

Beth was pointing to the receptionist's arms and fingers that were covered in the most exquisite, silver jewellery.

"Thanks," the receptionist beamed. "It's what I do when I'm not working here. You should come see my studio. I'm Ariana, by the way."

Beth instantly felt that they could be friends. Weird. That didn't usually happen. It generally took Beth a little time for her defences to disarm.

"Great to meet you, Ariana. Thanks, I definitely will."

Ariana showed Beth to her room. She was the only one staying at the pub that evening and Ariana had given her the suite. Suite. It was a large shabby double with a stained bedspread. But, it did have a huge bay window. Beth looked out at the harbour and the sea beyond. The decor was forgotten.

She sat at the window watching the sun melting into the sea.

Evan wasn't wrong. The place was beautiful.

Once it had set she jumped into the shower. And after fifteen delicious minutes being sprayed clean in the steaming water, she threw herself back onto the large bed, still wrapped in a towel; exhausted.

Her mind drifted and she slipped into a sweet dream of the sea and of a certain ripped, handsome kayaker with broad, muscular shoulders coming out of the water.

Only now he was topless and wearing a pair of tight black James Bond-style trunks that complimented his tight rear curves in a way she longed to dream about some more.

CHAPTER 3

----------✳---------

T he next day Beth woke up late. She wasn't sure if it was the long car journey or the sea air that had wiped her out, but she'd slept ten hours straight.

After a lazy morning, she found her way to Freshwater Bay Chapel for Evan's funeral.

She spent most of her time in chef whites and didn't have much in the way of what she called 'civvies', but she'd found a black slip dress at the back of her wardrobe and a pair of black heeled sandals which she vowed to change as soon as she could after the service.

In the chapel, she was ushered to a seat near the back, where thankfully she saw a familiar face.

Ariana smiled and beckoned her over.

"This is my gran, Gwen. "

Beth nodded to her as she sat down alongside them in the pew.

Ariana handed her an order of service. Her lips curled as she watched Beth trying to decipher the Welsh.

"Evan Morgan was a friend of mine in London," Beth explained.

"That's why you're here. We were wondering."

"We?"

"A pretty young stranger turns up on her own out of season, it gets noticed," Ariana whispered. "Someone was asking about you, that's all."

"Really?"

Beth coloured up.

"Uh-huh."

"Evan and me. We're both chefs. We liked talking about food and stuff."

Did Ariana think it odd?

"He was a lovely man," she added defensively. "He had some great stories."

"That he did," Gwen agreed.

She gave Beth a quirky smile.

"And I can see why he liked you."

The congregation quietened. The immediate family came in and sat in the reserved pews at the front.

Ariana bent her head towards Beth.

"Thank you for coming all this way."

The place was packed to the gills. The organ began a sombre hymn and from the back of the chapel, four men carried the polished wooden coffin down the aisle.

Beth caught her breath. The bearer at the front of the coffin. It was the kayaker.

The service was all in Welsh, and to its strange lyrical tones Beth's mind and eyes kept drifting.

Studying him from afar, the kayaker was as handsome as she remembered. More so, in his sharp black suit. But his strong jawline and deep-set eyes made him look stern. Impenetrable.

When the service ended, Evan was laid to rest beside Monique in the hillside graveyard, overlooking the sea.

Afterwards, the congregation gathered in the community hall for the funeral tea. The whole village and beyond had turned up it seemed. And Beth was surprised that they all appeared to know each other.

Volunteers poured out strong tea from giant battered metal teapots into cup after cup for the guests. And Beth was impressed by the huge homemade buffet stretching out along tables to the side. Plate upon plate of freshly cut sandwiches, sausage rolls, sponge cakes, scones and buttered bara brith, a

Welsh tea bread that Beth immediately wanted the recipe for.

Touching Beth's arm, Ariana guided her towards a tall, older gentleman, and a striking, rather intimidating woman in a stiff, black dress and pearls. They were surrounded by a crowd, but Ariana worked her and Beth politely through.

"David is Evan's brother," she whispered to her.

Ariana caught Ellen's eye.

"Ellen, David. Can I introduce Beth to you? She's Evan's friend from London. A chef."

Beth wished the ground would swallow her up whole. It was bad enough that she couldn't understand a word of the funeral. But now everyone was staring at her.

She felt her cheeks burning bright red as Ellen reached out unexpectedly and gave her a warm embrace.

"David, this is the famous Beth."

"You know who I am?"

"Of course. Evan was always talking about you. He raved about your food. Which, my dear, is quite a compliment."

Beth swallowed the lump in her throat. The funeral was sad, but hearing her talk about Evan like that, it was the first time she'd felt close to tears.

"I'm sorry for your loss."

Ellen was gushing, but there was something about the woman that made Beth feel like she was being assessed carefully as they spoke.

Nevertheless, she couldn't let this moment pass without tackling what had been gnawing away at her.

"Do you mind if I ask how he died? Who found him?"

They were being so nice to her now. But how would they be when they discovered that she hadn't been in touch with him? Being busy at work was a pathetic excuse.

Ellen cocked her head.

"Oh *gosh* dear, you didn't think he was in London, did you? He was here, with us."

A flood of relief washed over her.

"I thought he must've died on his own. I hadn't called be-

17

cause…"

Ellen cut across.

"He went peacefully in his sleep. Aneurysm, the doc said. It was a blessing. He had cancer. He didn't have that long."

"He never said."

"Played his cards close, did Evan."

She patted Beth's hand.

"Evan Morgan was a canny one. And he always said you kept him young at heart."

Beth smiled at her, weakly.

"Come and see us tomorrow, " Ellen pressed on. "Come for lunch. The pub'll give you directions to the farm. We'll have a proper chat then."

Beth agreed just as a large lady squeezed past her to give her condolences, edging Beth slowly out from the throng.

Watching them all chatting together in large groups in Welsh, Beth suddenly felt very alone. An outsider who didn't belong there.

Holding her cup of tea and the plate of food she had no appetite for, she scanned the room for Ariana, the only person that she knew.

But Ariana by now was deep in conversation, holding court with a large gathering of friends around her and a baby in her arms.

That's when she spotted him again.

In the middle of them all was the sexy, stony-faced kayaker, who she now saw bore a strong resemblance to Ellen.

He had to be one of Evan's nephews. Maybe the one who's girl-friend had died? Was that his baby that Ariana was holding?

Horrified, in that same second his eyes caught Beth's with a penetrating stare.

It made her heart bounce and gave her the jolt she needed to get the Hell out of there.

CHAPTER 4

----------✳--------

H e'd sat all Sunday evening nursing a pint of real ale at the Lobster Pot hoping to meet the alluring blonde. But she never showed.

He'd asked about her as he waited at the bar, but Ariana could only tell him that she was from London and staying for four nights.

Then, he'd seen her at the funeral.

She'd been sitting next to Ariana and Gwen in the chapel, so they were bound to have found out more about her.

Gareth had been edging his way across the hall to Ariana to winkle out more details when he saw that the mysterious hot guest was looking his way. In fact, she was staring directly at him.

Had it been too obvious that he was interested in her? Or was it her, checking him out?

Their eyes met for a moment before she turned shyly away.

But Gareth's eyes lingered. Her black dress showed off her long, golden curls and made her slim figure look fragile. Or was it the way she was standing? She seemed uncomfortable.

He was right. She felt out of place. Putting her plate of untouched food on a trestle table she slipped away, disappearing out the back of the hall.

She'd made his heart thump. But he was still none the wiser who she was.

The meeting with the solicitors was in half an hour and Ariana was still chatting with old friends, cuddling Jake. In fact, she hadn't paused for breath so far. He'd no chance of speaking to her alone, now. It would have to keep.

Leaving the hall too, he set off up the hill to the clifftop restaurant and his meeting with the solicitors.

The climb was steep, but not far. And he welcomed the fresh air and exercise after the sandwiches and cake he'd eaten.

Poor Uncle Evan. Gareth had spent many a weekend as a teenager up to his elbows in soapy water, washing dishes in the restaurant. Evan had tried to teach him to cook, but it was soon obvious that Gareth's talents lay elsewhere. He was happy enough prepping the vegetables and cleaning the plates.

What an amazing chef Evan had been. And lovely Auntie Monique, front of house keeping the customers happy. She was always spoiling him with a glass of coke or ice cream. Happy days.

He hoped this meeting wouldn't take long. The formal response, no doubt, from his uncle's estate. Confirming what he already knew; the property would be sold.

Mr Davies, the solicitor was getting out of his large BMW as he reached the restaurant car park.

He shook Gareth's hand and then went to open the rear car door. A set of familiar legs stretched out from it. Shapely, slender and bare. He'd noticed them earlier, at the funeral tea.

"Gareth Morgan, this is Beth Barnes. Beth will be joining us for the meeting."

Beth's eyes widened.

The kayaker.

Gareth Morgan? He wasn't the single father, after all. This was Evan's eldest nephew. The architect.

And he was studying her like he was examining an insect.

She cringed. Had he seen her checking him out?

Feeling her cheeks flush, she directed her attention towards the solicitor.

"Thank you for the lift."

The solicitor went to unlock the restaurant doors.

It was obvious that Le Gallois had been shut for a long while. The air was stale, the surfaces dusty. But Beth could see beyond the cobwebs.

She'd heard so much about this place.

"Do you mind if I take a look around?"

She surprised herself with the request. She wasn't usually this forward.

The solicitor gave a sweeping gesture as if the place was his.

"Be my guest."

She imagined what the place had been like in its heyday. A French seaside brasserie.

Covering the walls were old French advertising posters. Intimate navy leather booths gave privacy to the space, and the full-length windows facing out to the sea gave the most amazing views of the bay.

She drifted towards the prep area and took in the large kitchen with fairly modern equipment, fridges and stoves still in place. Nothing had been sold off. Evan had simply shut the door and walked away.

Sitting at one of the booths, Gareth watched her as she drifted around the restaurant.

Who was she?

A dawning realisation crossed his mind. She was obviously Evan's mistress.

The wily old fox. He'd never have thought his uncle had it in him.

She'd probably been fleecing him good and proper.

He ground his teeth and removed his tie.

Beth Barnes, the petite blonde who'd put him under a spell too and wasted his whole evening. What charms had this beautiful little fortune hunter used to dupe his dear old uncle?

He bet that she'd wrapped those silky, smooth legs around him. Let him touch her long, soft, golden curls. Fluttered her eyelashes seductively and asked him to leave her his restaurant.

And that was what she was up to now. Wandering around. Nosing about in the kitchen. Valuing the assets.

He could feel the hackles on the back of his neck rising as he waited to get this over with. Hear how his dreams of the eco-development had been dashed by this bewitching blonde gold digger.

The solicitor cleared his throat loudly, drawing Beth back to the meeting.

She sat down in the booth next to the solicitor, across from Gareth.

He kept his gaze impassive. Staring straight at her, steeling himself to see how things were likely to unfold, now that he knew her game.

How could she do that? With his old uncle. It was one step up from prostitution.

Disconcerted by his fierce, uncompromising glare, Beth sat down at the booth next to the solicitor.

The man she'd dreamed about the night before, now faced her. His dark hair was tousled from the walk. It was the only rebellious feature of this flinty-faced statue.

"Well, I'm sure you're wondering about the purpose of this meeting," the solicitor began a little pompously.

"I'm here to inform you of Evan Morgan's last wishes and the details of his estate."

"Hold on. Shouldn't my father be here?"

The stony statue spoke.

"Mr Morgan, as Executor, there will be other settlements in due course. As you may be aware, Evan Morgan's London property needs to be sold. But the specific contents I wish to discuss with you today relate to yourself and Miss Barnes here. Therefore, *if you wouldn't mind,* I'd like to continue."

Beth's lips curled in spite of her best efforts.

Gareth shifted uncomfortably but didn't respond.

"And so," the lawyer began again. "It is the wishes of Mr Evan Morgan that his property and land in Freshwater Bay are to go jointly and equally to Mr Gareth Morgan and Miss Beth Barnes. This includes the title of Le Gallois restaurant and the title of the adjacent hundred acres. These are bequeathed on the proviso that the aforementioned recipients use the property as a commercial restaurant and the land as outlined in the enclosed property development proposal written by Mr Gareth Morgan."

Beth let out a squeak.

Holy Macaroni!

Had she just heard right? Good Ol' Evan had left her the restaurant.

She composed herself.

Gareth Morgan glared coldly at her again, making her skin prickle.

The solicitor peered at each of them in turn over his glasses.

"However, my client did insist on including a caveat."

He began reading again.

"This property was cherished by the deceased because of the love that he found there with his late wife. Therefore, the aforementioned property will only be bequeathed in full if both Mr Gareth Morgan and Miss Beth Barnes have found partners and are married within twelve months of the deceased's date of death. In the event that either party remains unmarried at this time, the estate in Wales will be donated to the Crown. In the interim period, both parties will have full access to the property Le Gallois and the adjacent land where they may begin their plans at their own risk."

There was a long pause.

Had she just heard correctly?

Gareth was glowering at the solicitor.

"You're joking, right? You can't tell me that's legal?"

NELL GREY

The solicitor removed his glasses and wiped them with a small cloth from his pocket.

The deceased apparently could do what he liked. And if they didn't like it, they didn't have to accept.

"*Whoa...* hold on."

Beth spoke for the first time. She was still taking all of this in.

"So... if I don't get hitched, *he* can't keep the property either, *right*?"

She glanced at Gareth across the table. His flinty eyes unnerved her.

The solicitor shuffled his papers.

"Yes. And vice versa."

He quickly stowed the will back into his briefcase.

"I'm sure you've got lots to discuss together. The property is yours until next March, so I'll leave you the keys. That's all I can help you with at the moment, I'm afraid. You'll both need to inform me of... *uh...* any changes to your marital status over the next few months, of course."

He rose from the booth.

"Now, if you'll excuse me, I'll leave you to it. Quite a remarkable man. And a most unusual will."

Beth was reeling. She had to get married to get the restaurant. How on earth was that going to happen?

"So, what's the story, then?"

His angry sneer cut through the dusty air.

Hit by his intimidating tone, Beth turned her attention back to Gareth.

His mouth was clenched and he was glaring stonily at her.

"I said, what's the story?"

She tried to hold her chin high, determined not to flinch.

"How does some tempting little gold digger from, from where? London? Get gifted a million-pound restaurant?"

She couldn't believe what he was suggesting. And he wasn't done yet.

"Whatcha have to do for it? Flash those beautiful green eyes of yours and say *let me have your restaurant, you gullible, old Welsh*

24

fool."

Hold on.

He was insinuating that she was having some kind of affair with Evan. And worse than that, as bad-minded as that was, he was accusing her also of tricking him. Like she was some criminal con artist.

"How dare you."

She saw his dark brows slamming together, scowling at her response. Daring to defy him.

Her mouth was dry but she was pleased that she got the words out. She was shaking with anger but she was still in control.

"Listen, you *misogynistic arsehole*; you know nothing about me."

She continued, even though she could see that he was fuming. Who the Hell did he think he was?

"Don't look at me like that, Mr High and Mighty. You're set to get your paws on half of it too."

His eyes drilled into her, but she glared back at him. Daring him to say more.

Instead, he remained stubbornly silent. So, she hit him with the sucker punch.

"With such a lousy view of women, good luck finding a wife... I have it on good authority, now deceased, that your last girlfriend dumped you for your best mate."

She made a play of looking him up and down; slowly, deliberately and dismissively.

"And I can totally see why."

The stinging comment was out there now, hanging between them.

Gareth's face was expressionless and cold.

"My wife... It was my wife that, as you so gently put it, *dumped me.*"

He paused.

"My *ex*-wife."

Silence enveloped them.

He stared at her lividly.

Her heart was beating furiously. She was unwilling to add more to what could not be unsaid. But no way was she apologising, either. She had to tough this one out.

He hurled her a final, sardonic look.

"I guess we're done here."

He rose from the booth and strode away.

"Gareth Morgan," she called after him. "I never asked for any of this. Believe me."

He slammed the restaurant door behind him.

"Though I'm sure you don't."

The keys lay on the table in front of her. It was a complete and utter mess.

Without warning, she wept. She cried for Evan. She cried about Gareth's impression of her as some geriatric-loving money-grabber. She cried about the way he'd set her pulse racing even though she hated him.

But most of all, she cried because she wanted this place. It was beyond anything she had ever dreamed of. But she knew she could never have it.

She couldn't do what was being asked of her. And she may as well go over to the solicitors in the morning, hand back the keys and go back to London. And that would be that.

Unlocking the door onto the deck that wrapped around the restaurant, the fresh air cooled her feverish face and she wiped her tears away with her hand.

Why had Evan done this to her? It was like someone putting a feast of the most delicious food in front of you and then snapping it away before you could taste it.

And as for Mr Poker Up His Arse, she wouldn't speak to him again, even if her heart still pounded when she thought about him.

She needed to explain about the will to Evan's brother, David. She'd set the record straight. And maybe they would see who she really was and understand why she couldn't go through with it.

But *oh!* this place. It was wonderful.

She couldn't stay here one more minute. If she did, she'd never leave.

Closing the restaurant door behind her, she locked up her impossible dream.

It was only as she tottered in her heels down the hill to the harbour that she remembered. He'd said she had beautiful eyes.

CHAPTER 5

----------✳︎---------

"**A**aarrggghhh!"
Gareth shouted into the wind.
He stomped along the boathouse deck, and grabbing an old deckchair, slammed himself into it.

He stewed on what had happened, staring blankly out at the sea.

Why was he so hopping mad?

Was it the terms of the will? Or was it the way she'd stood up to him? The way she'd thrown his failed marriage in his face.

What had she called him? A misogynistic arsehole. *Yeah, right.* He was just calling it as he saw it.

She knew how to press his buttons. The understated, shy veneer and the feisty fighter underneath. Beth Barnes was certainly a piece of work.

Uncle Evan, let's face it, he was an easy mark. A vulnerable old man alone in a big city. He was the perfect target for a beautiful, young con artist who sold him a line and listened to his stories.

She'd done her homework. Found about the family, about him too.

So, if she was a clever fraudster, why did he feel so bad?

She looked genuinely shocked when he called her out. But then, she'd hissed back at him like an alley cat. And she hadn't backed down either.

Staring out at the sea and the islands calmed him.

Whatever personal stuff Evan had blabbed about him, it wasn't the full story. She hadn't known he'd been married. Or divorced. *Dammit!*

He had a year to find a new wife if he wanted to keep the land and do the development project. How was that even legal?

A business idea was one thing, but there was no way he was going back there and getting shackled to the wrong woman again.

He was done with bad relationships. Yep, he way preferred being Mr Shallow. Mr One Night Stand with tourists. Bar-room hook-ups. No drama. No rows. No heartache.

But there was no denying it. This was a lifetime opportunity. He'd never have the chance again to build the eco-chalets he'd designed. He'd never be able to find a development plot like this without a multi-million-pound price tag.

It didn't matter how he squared it, his uncle's terms couldn't be met. And honestly, after the nightmare of Chantelle, he'd never get himself imprisoned in another loveless lie of a marriage.

He'd see Beth tomorrow and apologise to her for what he'd said. Whether she'd been after Evan's money or not, she was right. He had been an arsehole to her. And sexist in the conclusions he'd jumped to about her.

He grinned, remembering her feisty eyes flashing at him.

Hopefully, if he could explain himself she'd understand why she couldn't have Le Gallois either.

Beth hardly slept a wink. She lay in bed picturing Le Gallois open again with her as Head Chef and owner. And she visualised the dishes she'd create.

It would be a mid-range French-inspired restaurant with a seafood speciality. It would be like in France, where whole families would go on Sundays to eat together and while away the afternoon. This could be her big break, her opportunity to do something amazing with her life.

How hard could it be to find a man?

Mr Right had eluded her so far. But surely, she could talk to one of the chefs back in La Vie and they could come in with her. Treat it like a project? Gary was always hanging around her.

She dismissed that idea quickly. No one would marry her without expecting something more. The thought of Gary touching her made her feel queasy.

It was no good. It felt like she was prostituting herself for a pipe dream. And that wasn't right.

In spite of everything, she couldn't help but feel annoyed with Evan for putting her in this situation. Gareth had called her a gold digger, a manipulator. But the truth was, it was Evan, from his freshly covered grave who was holding all the power over her. And over Gareth too.

And whatever she thought about Gareth, he must be feeling rotten about it all. Having to find another wife, when he was still obviously raw about his first one. She'd thrown *that* in his face like a custard pie.

Mr Arrogant had so deserved it, though. He clearly hated her. So, there was no point discussing anything further with him.

Beth got up early. It was madness to even contemplate it, considering it was spring and the Irish Sea would be freezing cold. But, she'd promised herself in London, whatever the weather she was going for a swim.

Dressed in her costume with her running clothes over the top and a towel in a small backpack, she headed out from The Lobster Pot Inn and jogged up the hill to Le Gallois as dawn broke.

She paused for breath as she reached the car park. In her pocket were the keys. She held them in her hand but couldn't bring herself to put them in the lock.

Instead, she strolled around the side of the restaurant. She hopped over onto the deck at the restaurant's front, facing out to the sea.

The waves were calm again today and the water was a deep turquoise blue. Perfect for a swim.

She gazed out at the cliffs of the peninsula to the south of her. This place had a tremendous view.

Below her, at the base of the rocks and over to the right was a grey boathouse with a high deck around it and a slipway down to the sea. There was no car there.

She was sure that no one would mind if she left her bag on the slipway. It would stay nice and dry on that deck.

Buoyed up by the idea, Beth took off and made her way down the track to the boathouse.

She'd been right. She walked onto the deck. The place was empty. Most likely, a holiday home.

Checking around again and seeing no one about, she quickly took off her clothes, and... *whoa!* She suddenly found herself shimmying out of her swimsuit too.

She never did anything spontaneous and wild. And here she was. Naked. Standing on the slipway with the water below. A secret fantasy.

The place was private. And it felt so thrilling. So naughty.

Summoning up the courage to go for it, she stood for a couple of minutes pondering whether this was indeed a wise thing to do.

It was now or never.

Steeling herself, she dived smoothly into the cold, blue sea.

She'd heard some Scandinavians bathed naked every day and she could see why. The immediate intoxicatingly painful shock as she plunged into the freezing water charged her full of endorphins.

She splashed around and bent her head back. The chilly, rippling waters easing all the worries from her mind. She felt cleansed by the sea. Blissful and positive in the rush stimulated by the icy cold.

It would all be fine, the sea told her.

After a few minutes, the temperature of the water began to bite and it was time to get out.

Embarrassed for the first time, she scanned the boathouse and shoreline. Then, easing herself out onto the slipway she scrambled onto the deck. Grabbing her things she hastily wrapped herself in the towel.

She tensed up.

She sensed someone about.

Did something move inside the boathouse?

Slowly, she turned her head, dreading seeing a face at the window.

But the boathouse was deserted.

She exhaled deeply.

Still a little spooked, she battled to get her clothes on. The lycra sports gear sticking stubbornly to her wet body.

Then, fixing her hair back into a ponytail she jogged quickly up the hill, past the restaurant and down to the Lobster Pot Inn for a hot shower and some poached eggs for breakfast.

Gareth couldn't believe what he had just seen. He thought he was about to be busted, but luckily he'd gotten away with it.

After the solicitor's meeting, he'd sat outside for hours on the boathouse deck mulling over his options, drinking whisky from a bottle he'd been saving.

He'd sat there until way too late, and then he'd fallen asleep on the old couch he'd put there while he was renovating.

It had been an inspired decision to stay over. Because this morning, he'd woken up to a new view. One even better than the islands. A set of shoulders covered in a curtain of golden curls.

It was her.

A slim waist, shapely hips and rounded buttocks. His mouth went dry as he was transfixed by her beauty.

He was suspicious at first. She'd found out he had the boathouse, and she was doing this to taunt him, or trap him.

But seeing how twitchy she was, looking around, he changed

his mind.

No. He was certain she had no idea he was watching. Or that the boathouse was his.

She stood on the slipway for ages. Just as he thought she was going to bottle it, she lifted her feet and sprang into a neat dive, plunging into the sea below.

The water was cold at this time of the year. He hoped she knew what she was doing. He didn't fancy fishing her out.

Luckily, she seemed at ease in the water. And he moved back, out of sight as she climbed from the sea.

That image of her standing facing him was seared on his eyes like a cattle brand.

He'd hoped to God she wouldn't peer in through the windows. To be sure, he'd ducked well out of sight until he was completely certain she was gone.

His head was filled with Beth Barnes. Again.

CHAPTER 6

----------*---------

When Beth got back to the Lobster Pot Inn, Ellen had left her a message with directions to the farm. She was holding firm on the promised lunch date.

The swim had invigorated her and helped to put some perspective on recent events. She'd decided she had to get in touch somehow with Gareth.

She was going to enjoy slapping him down once and for all. Letting him know in no uncertain terms that Evan was not her sugar daddy and he'd not be going ahead with his project because there was no way she was getting married any time soon.

By the time she'd walked the mile or so to the farm, she'd thoroughly convinced herself of her intentions. She was early for lunch but she didn't have much else to do, so she figured that Ellen wouldn't mind if she lent a hand.

The day was a little too warm for her navy sweater, jeans and boots, but she'd made sure that she was conservatively dressed. She didn't want Ellen and David also thinking she was some strumpet. Evan's mistress! It was ridiculous.

Cae Môr Farm was hard to miss. The farmhouse was solid stone and imposing. The gravel courtyard was littered with pots of spring flowers. There were large modern sheds and brand-new tractors on the yard. The Morgans were not some two-bit smallholders.

Two border collies came out to greet her on the driveway.

They appeared friendly enough but Beth was wary. She'd not had much to do with dogs beyond the small groomed fur babies she saw in London.

"Oh, hi Beth. Come on in, love. Don't mind those two. Soft as brushes, they are."

Ellen gave her a warm hug and took her through to her large, farmhouse kitchen.

Beth thought that Ellen looked far less intimidating than she had at the funeral. But she had the same strong jaw and deep-set eyes as Gareth.

She checked herself. Could she not have two minutes without him seeping into her thoughts?

She noticed the mixing bowl on the table.

"What you making?"

"Well, seeing as you're a chef," Ellen explained a little flustered. "I was trying out this new recipe I got off the internet for a chicken pie. But look, I've gone and totally messed up the pastry. Please come and help me save it."

Beth laughed as Ellen threw her hands into the air.

Looking at the pastry, it was indeed ruined. It had been overworked.

Ellen shrugged resignedly and handed her an apron while Beth rolled up her jumper sleeves.

"Don't worry. I'm sure it'll be lovely."

She washed her hands.

"May I?"

Ellen handed her a teaspoon and Beth tasted the filling.

"That's so good. I think I'll be getting this recipe."

Ellen puffed up a little at that. And while she was at the stove, Beth discreetly put the pastry to one side.

"How about some filo? Make it into a Greek pie."

"Ooh, that sounds lovely."

Ellen watched on as Beth made a stiff dough and kneaded it steadily, adding a couple more spoons of olive oil as she worked. She made it look easy as she cut the dough into small balls and covered them with cling film to rest.

Ellen handed Beth some tea in a china mug with a puffin on it.

"You've saved me from disaster and I don't mind admitting it."

"We'll need to do some pretty fancy rolling. But I'll show you how, and if you like this pastry, you can try it out on your friends. Certainly goes down well at the restaurant."

Beth helped Ellen clean up. She was enjoying her company.

They chatted about Evan and London, and Ellen told her about the family. She insisted on adding her as a Facebook friend and made Beth promise she'd come and see them again.

Beth wasn't feeling brave enough to bring up the details of the will yet, so she let Ellen run on about the boys growing up on the farm. It sounded idyllic.

"We're going to need a long thin rolling pin for the filo. You don't have anything we could use lying around, d'you?"

Ellen re-appeared a couple of minutes later with a long piece of wooden dowling, an offcut from a craft project.

"Perfect."

Beth rolled up the sleeves of her rather tight navy sweater, which was now a little floury. Taking each dough ball in turn, she skilfully pressed down on each end of the dowling flattening out the ball and then stretching the pastry sideways.

Rolling and stretching, she worked the pastry expertly until they were each paper-thin, oiled and laid out carefully on a baking tray on top of each other.

"Come on Ellen, why don't you have a go at it?"

"Oh, my goodness, no. You carry on rolling, love. I know when I'm out of my depth."

Gareth watched on in awe. Like the pastry, Ellen was being worked by a master.

His mother mouthed a 'hello' as she saw him slipping quietly into the kitchen, filling the door frame. She said that he only ever came to see them at mealtimes. That was true.

But he'd never have come if he'd have known she'd be in the kitchen giving his mother a cookery lesson.

His mother. The best Victoria sponge baker in Pembrokeshire, according to her.

This was interesting, to say the least.

Beth carried on assembling the pie.

"Voila!"

Ellen gave her a clap as Beth slid it into the oven, and in return, she gave Ellen a small bow.

His face twitched as he tried to suppress a smile. This woman kept surprising him.

But what was her game here, getting pally with his mother? She was obviously a talented chef and people instantly warmed to her.

But his mam was no fool. If she knew about the will she'd be having her doubts about Beth Barnes too.

He watched his mother fussing as Beth insisted on cleaning up. Her back was to the door, so when she turned she gave a gasp of surprise at seeing him standing there.

He unsettled her, he could tell. But then he saw her chin rise and she held his gaze, daring him to say something. Beth was still angry with him.

That same sparky defiance in her eyes amused him. It was like she was taunting him to challenge her again.

He'd be polite. Nothing more.

"Hi."

He saw his mother studying them curiously.

"You two know each other?"

Gareth pulled his eyes away from Beth.

"Yes. Uh... from the funeral."

He noticed how Beth shrugged nonchalantly. Was she trying to deny the tension oozing between them?

No way was he bringing Ellen up to speed with things. There was no reason for his parents to think badly of Evan.

He'd tell Beth that he had no intention of marrying and she'd go back to London. No one would ever know about the will.

He needed to talk with her. Alone.

He cleared his throat.

"Uh.. the pie. It'll take a while to cook? Why… why don't I show you around the farm? Mam, you'll keep an eye on the pie, right?"

Both women stared at him dubiously.

His heart had started up again. Beth looked amazing.

His mouth twitched. So, maybe he preferred his morning view of her.

A light dusting of flour on her navy jumper was flecked around the base of her breasts. She'd noticed the flour too and was trying to wipe it discreetly away. These were details he did not want to focus on.

Ellen gave him a quizzical look that mothers did when they wondered what their sons were up to.

Beth shrugged half-heartedly at him.

"Okay, then. Lead the way."

Ellen watched them go outside.

He was a good boy, that one. And there was no doubt that he fancied this English girl. The smouldering looks he was giving her. His tongue was all but hanging out.

It had been funny to watch. Gareth was always so reserved.

She'd not seen him like that before.

Even with Chantelle.

He'd been stepping on eggshells the whole time with that one. He never much talked much about it, and she let him be.

She'd never taken to Chantelle, anyway. He'd been far too good for her, she'd always said it. In the end, she was proved right. He was so much happier now he was back home.

The last thing Gareth needed was to be going after another city girl. And one like Beth, who anyone could see was headstrong and would tell him exactly what she thought.

What was wrong with the women here in Freshwater Bay? He needed a nice Welsh girl. Like that new teacher in the village. In her twenties, single. She'd be perfect.

She checked the pie. The layers of the pastry were puffing up beautifully.

No, Gareth needed to settle down here, not go traipsing off after some London chef who worked long hours and would soon get bored and leave him. Just like the last one had.

Gareth shook his head woefully at Beth's heeled suede boots. He walked with her silently around the animal sheds, trying to find the least muddy route for her.

He pointed brusquely into the lambing shed.

"Maternity ward."

The ewes were penned in, fat and happy. Some had their heads in a trough of feed. Others were sitting in the straw, chewing.

She wondered why he was bothering to do the tour. He was barely being civil.

She couldn't deny it, though. Gareth Morgan was hot. Even in his dirty work clothes. He'd been sawing wood, she could see bits of sawdust in his dark hair.

She quickly focussed, and remembered with some annoyance, what he'd hurled at her the day before.

The pen next door contained a ewe with new-born triplets. They moved stutteringly in their first hours of life. Their legs too long for their small woollen, wrinkled bodies.

She felt Gareth's eyes on her as she bent over the pen.

"They're so cute!"

Forgetting herself, she flashed Gareth a smile and sensed him thawing.

"I've never seen live ones up close before."

He looked at her incredulously.

"What? You've never seen a lamb? Did Evan know that?"

She threw him a look.

"No. I was too busy seducing him and conning him out of his money to talk about farming."

He cleared his throat.

"Fair enough."

He looked away huffily and she felt bad.

"Look, me and Evan. We were pals. That's it."

She wasn't convinced he believed her.

The atmosphere was polite enough but she could tell that both of them were feeling uncomfortable around each other. There was an awkward silence growing between them.

Gareth shuffled his feet, looking at the concrete floor of the shed.

He turned to face her.

"Beth, let's leave Mam and Dad out of this for now, eh? They don't need to know about the terms of the will and I don't want them to think badly of Uncle Evan. They're still grieving. D'you mind?"

"Course not," she stuttered, taken aback by his sincerity.

His eyes met hers, fiery now and intense.

"Thank you."

Trying to slow her racing pulse, she turned away. This was not the way she wanted her traitorous body to behave.

The last thing she wanted was Mr Up Himself to see her simpering all over him like some teenager with a crush.

As they wandered together out of the lambing shed back towards the farmhouse, she felt inexplicably disturbed. There was something about Gareth Morgan that unsettled her in a million different ways.

Was that why she hadn't told him that she was turning down the inheritance?

When Gareth returned to the kitchen with Beth, Ellen was serving up the most delicious melt-in-the-mouth chicken pie she had ever tasted. Not that she'd let Beth know that.

Throughout lunch, she saw how her son couldn't stop himself from sneaking looks as Beth chatted about the restaurant in

London and the celebrities she'd seen eating there. And she'd told her about her other son, Rhys. He'd probably been to her restaurant, when he was in London. And how he was in New York at the moment, filming. Beth was impressed.

She wasn't making eye contact with Gareth, but there'd been something going on between them. A mother's instincts were never wrong.

And by the looks of things, her son was back in the saddle, ready to move on. She'd sort that dinner invite as soon as she could.

After lunch, she heard Gareth offer to give Beth a lift back to the Lobster Pot in his truck, but Beth refused. She needed the fresh air and a walk after all that food she told them all as she left.

Ellen watched from the window as she disappeared down the driveway.

"What did you make of her, then?"

She studied her son carefully.

His sullen shrug made her heart sink. He fancied her.

Ellen cleared the plates off the table.

"Well, she'll be back in London soon enough."

Gareth got up and gave his mother a hand to clear the table.

"How close was she to Evan?"

Ellen wiped the table.

"Evan was always going on about her. He had a real soft spot for Beth, he did."

"He did?"

Ellen stopped wiping.

"No, you dope. Not in that way. Evan was mentoring her. Said she was the next big talent. Thick as thieves they were. I think she learned a lot off him."

Gareth went over to the window.

"What's up, son?"

"Ah, nothing."

He moved to the sink to start washing the dishes.

Ellen grabbed a tea towel.

"I was wondering, have you met the new schoolteacher? She

moved into the village in the autumn. I thought I might invite her around one evening for supper, if you're free?"

Gareth's face turned flinty.

"It's up to you what you do, Mam. But don't expect me to be there."

CHAPTER 7

----------✴--------

Gareth's mind wandered as he sanded the boathouse walls the next day. Beth at the farm. Beth diving into the water. Beth's green eyes flashing as she challenged him. Not surprising since he'd called her a money-grabbing whore. And then, her face when she'd seen the lambs. There'd been a naivety about her. Almost girlish.

But he could tell too that she was no push-over.

He considered what his mam had said about her and Evan. Now he knew her better, he could see the two of them getting along.

He owed her an apology.

He'd blown it. The first woman he'd fancied in so long he couldn't remember, and she hated his guts.

Finding his phone, he gave Ariana a call.

"When's Beth leaving?... Is she there now?... Oh... Do you know where she was going for a walk?... No, no message. I needed to catch up with her, that's all."

He washed his face and tried to brush the worst of the dust out of his hair. He was still in his filthy workwear, but this wasn't a date.

He picked up his coat. He had an idea where she'd be.

And when he got there, he wasn't wrong.

The door was unlocked and Beth was standing in the restaurant area looking out through the huge windows at the sea.

He took a deep breath and she turned around, startled to see him.

"I had to come here one last time," she explained. Her voice sounded a little sad.

She turned away from him.

"Beth, I need to apologise. I was out of order. I'm sorry for what I said about you and Evan."

She listened impassively, looking out of the window, making him all the more tongue-tied.

"I was surprised to see you at the meeting... And then the whole inheritance thing... and those terms, that really threw me and... and *then* when you said that about Chantelle... but I want you to know that I'm not... what did you call me?"

She stared at the sea, her mouth twitching.

"A misogynistic arsehole."

It curved into a smirk.

Gareth grinned.

"Ah. Yes."

She turned around and she caught his smile as he ploughed on.

"It was a terrible thing to say to you. And you were right. I was sexist. But I'm not a misogynist, honest."

"You're just an arsehole, then?"

Her face cracked and they both laughed a little nervously as their eyes met.

"What I mean to say is, I'm sorry. Can we start over?"

Beth hadn't expected an apology. Especially a heartfelt one like that.

"Yes," she answered a little breathlessly. "I'm sorry too. I shouldn't have said that about your ex-wife. It's none of my business and it was cruel."

She gazed up into his unfathomable eyes.

"I'm no gold digger, Gareth. Believe me, I'm as shocked about this as you are. Evan came into my restaurant Le Vie En Rose. Table twelve, two o'clock, every Friday. I used to cook for him.

We used to meet for coffee, wine and walks in the park. We both liked talking about food."

It sounded lame when she said it like that. But surprisingly, she cared about what he thought.

"Beth. I believe you."

He'd caught her off guard, and much to her horror she sniffed back a tear.

"You do?"

"Yes."

She glanced away. This was a bad business all round, and it was time to end it now.

"Gareth, I've made up my mind," she began, gathering up her courage. If she didn't get this out now, she might not ever.

"I don't want anything to do with Evan's will."

He cocked his head, willing her to explain.

"I'm not seeing anyone. And I've absolutely no intention of getting married to some random plonker, just so as I get my own restaurant. I'm sorry that I've ruined your inheritance plans too. Perhaps you can go talk to the solicitors?"

Gareth held her gaze.

"You sure?"

"Yeah."

There was a long pause as he considered it further.

"OK. Gimme your phone. Call me if you change your mind."

She handed it over to him, letting him input their contact details.

She put the phone back in her bag.

"Beth?"

He touched her shoulders lightly, shooting a shiver through her.

Turning towards him, she glimpsed for a moment a rawness in his eyes that disturbed and thrilled her in equal measure.

"You doing anything this afternoon?"

It wasn't what she expected to hear.

She shook her head.

"And you're still going back to London tomorrow morning?"

She nodded.

Gareth appeared to be considering things.

"Come for a walk with me. I want to show you something."

Gareth led her out to the restaurant car park. She followed him across the track to the boathouse and through the gate into the fields that swept over the brow of the hill and down towards the sheer cliffs beyond Freshwater Bay.

"This is Uncle Evan's land. I thought you might want to see it before you make any final decisions."

He was much more friendly with her now. That was a relief. The moody glowering had been too much for her to cope with.

As she spent a little time with him, she could see that he was naturally quiet. Thoughtful, even.

Beth gasped as she looked down at the vertical drops a few feet away.

"That's immense."

She ventured closer to the cliff edge and watched as a seabird reeled and spun in the wind, trying to land on a cliffside ledge.

Gareth suddenly grabbed onto her firmly and pulled her back towards the path.

"Careful, you're too close to the edge. These cliffs are really dangerous. And it's slippery."

He held on to her hand. She didn't pull it away or look at him as he held onto her, walking her back away from the cliff edge. And then they carried on, down to the lower fields which were more sheltered in the lee of the highest clifftop hill.

Gareth stopped in the middle of the lowest field and Beth moved from him, letting go of his hand as she gazed around her. He'd held onto her hand as they'd walked down from the cliff tops. He hadn't meant to but their closeness felt good.

He was winging it, but something told him he needed to pitch his vision to her.

"This is where I'd do my development."

She gazed around her at the sea and the fields.

"It's so tranquil here."

"The project was to build ten eco-chalets. They're out of sight of the village but there's still a sea view."

"And some families would live here all year round, you say?"

Gareth smiled.

"Yeah."

"Wow. It's so different to the city. I mean, obviously it is. But, the sky it's so big out here. Imagine growing up, seeing this every day."

She gazed across the open fields and out to the vast blue beyond stretching as far as her eyes could see.

"No shopping malls or multiplex cinemas out here."

Gareth echoed her thoughts.

She turned to him, surprised.

He nodded to her suede heeled boots

"But there is a path down to the sea. I don't want you to hurt yourself, though."

Beth smirked back.

"The hopeless townie will be fine."

"Then, give me your hand. Let me make sure you don't slip."

He held onto her as they took the steep sandy path down to the small stony inlet cut narrowly into the cliff.

Standing on the shale shoreline at the edge of the calm water Beth bent down and picked up a flat pebble.

"Is that a cave?" she asked, pointing upwards.

It was a round carved hole in the cliff face about six feet above the waterline.

"We used to climb up and play there as kids," Gareth answered. "Gets flooded though in the storms. "

She threw the pebble across the still waters and screwed her nose up as it dropped straight into the sea.

"Must've been magical growing up here."

"Yeah. Freshwater Bay's a great place to be a kid."

Gareth picked up a pebble and skimmed it, getting six bounces.

Grinning at him, she took it as a challenge, trying again. The pebble plopped into the waves first bounce.

He found her another flat pebble. As he handed it to her, he covered his fingers around hers.

"See, hold it flat like this."

He demonstrated the flick of his wrist and skimmed the stone in her hand. Another a perfect bouncer.

She tried, copying how he'd kept his hand flat.

The pebble bounced twice.

"Yey!"

Gareth's face cracked into a broad smile and he handed her another pebble.

"It suits you."

"What?"

"Smiling."

She tried another stone, but annoyingly it submerged with a sudden sunken plop.

She tossed her final pebble into the water.

"You win the stone skimming challenge."

He put his hand on her shoulder lightly to guide her back up the beach. His hand covered hers again, making sure she didn't trip on the rough track, he told her.

As they wandered together over the fields back towards the restaurant he explained his eco-designs and the ideas behind his sustainable, community build.

Gareth couldn't deny it, Beth Barnes intrigued him and he was sad when they reached the car park. He didn't want it to end.

"Goodbye, Gareth. I enjoyed this afternoon."

Her voice sounded flat as she released her hand from his.

He could see her eyes drawn to the restaurant.

"And you're off tomorrow?"

She nodded.

"Thanks for showing me your development project. I'm gutted for you that it's not going to happen."

"I'm sorry too about the restaurant."

She shrugged.

"C'est la vie."

She turned away from him, crossing the car park back down the hill towards the inn.

And that was it.

Ah, dammit! He couldn't leave it like this.

"Hey! Beth?"

She turned around.

"If I find a way around things, will you rethink your decision?"

She raised her hands questioningly and dropped him an infectious, broad smile that had him laughing as she waved him goodbye.

Gareth sighed.

The reality was, unless he could come up with a plan, she had no intention of trying to keep Le Gallois.

The eco-chalet project was doomed to never get off the drawing board and he'd carry on getting building jobs about the place. Still, it was worth it to be able to live in Freshwater Bay.

Beth sat on the bench by the sea wall looking out at the boats in the harbour. It was her final evening in Freshwater Bay.

Gareth Morgan confused her. He believed her now about Evan. He'd held her hand as they'd walked. Far longer than he needed to.

She looked down at her boots. They'd held up pretty well, considering.

When he looked at her, she couldn't deny it, he made her feel breathless. And his smile. It transformed his face. She wished he did it more.

Why did she care whether he smiled more or not? Tomorrow she was going back to reality. Her life in London.

But, what if he did find a solution to their inheritance problem? What would she do then?

CHAPTER 8

----------✳---------

Madog called in at the boathouse with Jake on his way back from town.

"Hey bro, how's it going? Look who I've brought with me for the grand tour."

"Hey, Jakee. How are you today?"

Gareth took Jake in his arms and lifted him high, making him squeal with delight.

"He still loves his Uncle Gareth."

Madog wandered around.

"You've been busy, mate."

The floors were nearly all sanded back and the mezzanine floor and staircase up to the master bedroom and its en-suite bathroom were in place.

Madog peered into what was going to be a second bedroom, utility room and bathroom at the back of the ground floor.

"Soon you'll be able to babysit for me."

"I'll have to fight Mam for him first."

They gave each other a knowing look and laughed.

"She's been banging on about that new teacher all afternoon. She thinks she'd be good wife material for you," Madog said, taking Jake back into his arms and sniffing his nappy.

"And she wonders why Rhys never comes home."

"Yip. I knew it was you, not your Uncle Gareth. Smelly boy."

Madog moved Jake onto his hip and reached down to his rucksack for nappies and wipes.

After changing Jake, they moved through to the main living area with its double-height ceiling and large bi-fold doors opening out onto the deck and the sea.

Gareth wanted a modern Scandinavian feel and so he'd kept the floors and ceilings in the original wood.

"Remind me, if I ever do this again to put carpet in. Stripping this old, dirty pine's been a bitch. And I haven't even started oiling it white yet."

Madog laughed.

"No pain, no gain, Mr Architect. Just think of the workout those arms are getting. The staff at the village school will, no doubt, be very grateful."

Gareth gave his little brother a 'don't push it' look and a grin. It was great seeing Madog.

They made plans to go for a beer that weekend. The boy needed a bit of normality back in his life. Jake was a little cutey and had settled into a routine well. When the boathouse was done, he'd offer to have Jake for a night if Madog wanted to go and see his brother Owen in Cardiff.

It'd be good to give Mam a break too. He needed to have a serious word with her though, about not interfering in his life. He'd forgotten about how meddlesome she could be. It was one of the reasons he'd stayed in Manchester after university.

Later that evening after finishing up, he sat on the deck of the boathouse and cracked open a bottle of beer. It was his new favourite spot for his new favourite memory. Beth naked, diving into the water.

And after that, his second favourite memory. Beth getting out onto the slipway. And her skimming stones, trying to compete with him and getting annoyed when she failed.

What was going on?

He was losing the plot here. If he liked her that much, he should just call her. She'd be in the Lobster Pot now. There was nothing to stop them from hooking up for the night. She hadn't shrunk away when he'd held her hand.

He gazed up at the restaurant, sitting on the clifftop above the boathouse. Under the circumstances, suggesting a one night stand to Beth might not be the wisest idea. Especially after his first comments about her and Evan. Things were complicated enough.

He understood why Beth was walking away from the marriage clause. No one had to tell him how unhappy you could be if you married the wrong person, just because you felt pressured into doing it.

Chantelle had been a disaster from the get-go. He'd made the classic mistake. He'd got in too deep to get out.

Thinking back, he spent most of his time trying to please her. She'd fly off the handle over the smallest things. He'd liked Ariana's Facebook profile picture. That was followed by three days of accusations that he was having an affair. Pretty rich, when it was her who ended up cheating on him.

She'd hinted so badly and for so long about them getting married that he'd finally felt obliged.

There'd been two years of stag dos and weddings as all his university friends settled down, and he thought that it was time for him to do the decent thing too.

And so he proposed to her on Valentine's Day. Dinner for two and a diamond ring popped into the ice bucket with the champagne.

She'd said yes, on one condition. That they swapped the ring for one with a bigger stone.

That was so Chantelle.

So, no, he agreed with Beth. The terms of the will could not be met.

But, Dammit!

The inheritance was too good to let slip through their fingers. It felt wrong to simply walk away.

Beth hadn't said an outright 'no' when he asked her to let him try to find a way around the will.

He needed to consider the inheritance problem like an architect. When a building problem arose, he'd find the root cause and visualise things from other angles and perspectives.

There *had* to be a creative solution out there.

Despite a glorious sunset, no inspiration came.

And eventually, Gareth drove back to the harbour and his overnight digs on the boat.

The yacht was alright for a night or two, but he'd been living on it for a few months now and it was high time to go ashore.

He lay awake for hours on the small bed, thinking.

What could be done?

It was after three in the morning when it suddenly came to him.

How had he been so stupid?

He hastily jotted it down on a piece of paper. He would go straight to see Beth in the morning and fly it by her.

Finding peace at last, the lilting swell of the waves rocked him into a deep sleep from which he didn't wake until late the next morning.

CHAPTER 9

---------*---------

Beth was ready to leave first thing. She couldn't think of any way around the inheritance conundrum.

Creating a dish for a lactose-intolerant, gluten-free vegan with a peanut allergy, no problem. But this? The only answer she could think of was to walk away.

She'd been checking her phone all evening. She'd been secretly praying he might find an excuse to see her again. But she was obviously projecting her desires. She had a crush on him, that was all.

And her phone had remained stubbornly silent.

Gareth had given up on his dream too and had accepted what she'd said.

That was fair enough.

Plus it was what she had said she wanted.

So, why then did she feel so disappointed?

There was nothing more to say or do. She was up early and had checked out of the inn by nine the next morning.

She wanted to see Ariana before she headed off. If for no other reason than to thank her for making her feel so welcome at the funeral. She wasn't sure she would have stayed if she'd been all on her own.

With directions from the receptionist, she wandered into the village, passing the only shop and continuing up the road to a converted chapel, where she knocked tentatively on the heavy oak door.

There was no answer but she could hear music playing at full pelt inside.

"Knock knock," Beth called loudly as she opened the door.

Inside was not what Beth had expected at all.

The chapel had been gutted and painted a pure brilliant white; a light artistic space with all kinds of unusual artwork displayed.

Huge canvases of abstract art and more modest poster prints covered the high walls of the chapel between the long, thin paned windows. Mobile installations of coloured glass hung like chandeliers over where the pulpit had been.

There were subdivided sections across the floor space allocated to different artists, and these were set out as small exhibition areas with display cabinets full of glasswork, jewellery and ceramics.

The pieces were diverse, quirky and modern. Many used Celtic symbols and reflected abstractly the seascape and countryside of this beautiful part of Wales.

Ariana came out from a door at the back of the space.

"Beth! Great to see you. I'm so glad you came by before you left. Welcome to my world."

Ariana was dressed in a full-length paint-stained boiler suit with a pink bandana turban around her head, on top of which rested a set of safety goggles. Even in work clothes, she was artistic and cool.

"Who thought this place up? It's fantastic."

"You like it?" Ariana beamed. "They were closing the chapel a couple of years back and I knew it'd be perfect. Local artists get a space to display their art."

"I get a cut on each sale. It hardly covers the costs, hence the extra shifts at the Lobster Pot, but this place is my passion. Plus, I've a dealer in the States now who buys up the small pieces. It's the jewellery that's my thing."

Beth could tell that Ariana had a fantastic eye. She'd managed to bring an eclectic mix of art together so it had a similar vibe.

Beth was no expert. She was only a chef, but she liked it a lot.

"Wanna see *my* stuff?"

Ariana led her through to the back, where there were around fifty pieces of the most intricately worked Celtic silver jewellery Beth had ever seen.

Earrings, rings, necklaces and bangles; Ariana had taken the modern boho fashion and created Celtic designs which were light and could be worn as a set of bangles or as layered length necklaces.

"This is my summer collection," Ariana explained as Beth poured over them.

She could easily snap up at least five, even ten of the pieces. She loved the Celtic crosses layered into a necklace set and the pair of unusual climber earrings with a row of stars.

But of all the pieces, her eyes were drawn to a ring sat to one side of the display.

She touched it and held it up to examine it more closely.

"*Ahh.*"

Ariana grinned at her.

"This is special. It's a Welsh love ring and the design's meant to have Celtic powers. When a man puts this on your finger, he gives his heart to you. Lucky girl that gets this ring. It's full of passion."

She winked at her and laughed. The ring was made up of intricate filigree work in rose gold that wrapped around as a band.

"See that there," she showed Beth, "That's the Celtic Tree of Life. Love's like a tree with deep roots connecting you to your place. And the branches, that's where you blossom with only the sky as your limit."

"That's so beautiful. Can I try it on?"

Beth placed it on her ring finger, a perfect fit.

A cold shiver ran through her and she pulled it off immediately.

"You seriously should get a London dealer looking at these, Ariana. They'd go down an absolute storm."

Ariana shrugged.

"I s'pose. But I got shafted by a dodgy art dealer when I first started out. I'm still owed five grand, which I'm never going to see again. So, I'm quite picky about who I deal with. And I always insist on payment upfront."

She could have stayed all day chatting but she needed to get going.

With a hug and an invitation to stay any time in London, Beth left Ariana and headed back to her car. It was going to be a long journey home.

There was no doubt that Freshwater Bay had worked its magic on her too. And if she could, she would stay here forever.

Pulling out of the pub car park, she peered up at the restaurant on the clifftops. Le Gallois had been a lovely dream and she would always appreciate Evan's generosity. But a dream it was.

Gareth emerged onto the deck of the sailboat. It was half past ten; shockingly late time for a working man to be getting up on a Wednesday morning. But he'd not slept until after three, and these days he never bothered with an alarm.

Coffee in hand, he read over his notes from the night before. There in black and white was his brilliant idea.

In the cold light of day, was it so inspired? He wasn't so sure. It could work, but would she go for it? He wouldn't blame her if she didn't, after how he'd first treated her. She'd be quite right to still hate his guts, although he was sure she didn't. Not after their walk yesterday. He hoped she felt that they could be friends.

He'd go over and broach it to her before she left for London.

He looked across to where her car was parked.

The pub car park was empty.

He checked again, looking for any sign of her car parked up on the road or up at the restaurant.

His heart sank. The little silver Toyota was gone.

Argh!

He blew out a deep breath and stretched his arms behind his

head. He was too late.

Or was he?

He had one shot left and nothing to lose.

What the heck. He'd do it.

Opening his phone case, he began typing.

It took ages. He was trying to get the tone right and his large fingers were not made for mobile technology. Plus, the damn thing kept auto-correcting into random words, which was driving him nuts.

And how exactly was he going to write the proposal down like he wasn't coming on to her?

There needed to be no misunderstandings.

Finally, he was happy with what he'd written.

Grimacing, he pressed send.

He gulped down a mouthful of lukewarm, black coffee, feeling a little nauseous.

The tick by the side of the message confirmed that it had been delivered.

He'd found a solution to the will.

But his future was in her hands.

CHAPTER 10

----------*---------

I t took her eight hours to get back to London. The motorway had massive hold-ups and her car's engine started to
overheat, forcing her to stop at a service station. And then,
to top it all, the afternoon traffic into London was crazy.

It was now early evening and all Beth wanted was a bath, a
chicken pad thai takeaway and a hot chocolate. In that order.

As she shuffled around her tiny apartment, everything was de-
pressingly familiar. If she'd felt dissatisfied before she headed
out to Wales, now it was ten times worse.

She put it down to tiredness, hormones, post-travel blues,
whatever else she could think of, and started to run a bath.

Soaking in the hot tub, covered in bubbles she dreamed about
her restaurant by the sea. About the quaint, white cottages lining the harbour and the dramatic clifftops where Gareth had
held her hand to keep her safe.

Gareth. He was invading her thoughts again.

She'd promised to call her friends Alys and Jo. What would they
say about the will and her decision? She hoped they'd tell her
that she'd done the right thing. If they told her she'd been a fool
to give it up, she'd cry.

Her own restaurant. She was beginning to wonder if she had
been a fool.

She got out her Macbook and video called them. A long chat
and a giggle was just what she needed to lift her spirits.

La Vie had been manic and Alys had been working long hours. Jo was trying to persuade her bosses to do more serious journalism, instead of clickbait. She was sick of running ageing celebrities and skateboarding dog stories.

Beth told them about the funeral and about Freshwater Bay. But she kept the details about the will and the restaurant to herself. Neither did she tell them about Gareth. There was, after all, nothing to tell.

They arranged to meet up over the weekend, which was a real treat as she didn't get many weekends off. And hardly any with Alys off too.

Suddenly her phone, charging on the floor clicked on and pinged.

A message. From Gareth.

'I've been thinking about the will and the problem we both have. It seems a damn shame to throw these business opportunities away. You know my circumstances. A relationship is the last thing I want. And judging by what you said yesterday, you feel the same way. I have a proposal to make. A strictly business one. These are the terms:

a. We get married purely as a business arrangement.

b. The marriage will remain confidential.

c. When either of us wants out, we will both agree to a divorce. (You keep the restaurant? I keep the land?)

The restaurant has an apartment above it. I'll be living in the boathouse. So, we can lead separate lives. No one but us will know.

Will you marry me, Beth?

Gareth'

She read it again, and then about five times more.

He'd certainly thought through the details, even the divorce settlement.

The message was sent just after ten that morning. It had been twelve hours and she hadn't responded. He must be sweating it out, wondering what she'd say.

She smirked to herself. Good.

Wow! Big question. Was she prepared to marry a man who could be so bad-minded and sexist? So aloof, so closed off, so annoyingly intimidating, unfathomable and... and... a man she *so* had the hots for.

Was she being fair to him? Her turning up was a shock. And he'd made a big effort to apologise afterwards. He'd been so sincere, his words had touched her.

She'd enjoyed the afternoon they'd spent together. He'd been nice to her and considerate. He'd worried about her on the cliffs, he'd taught her to skim stones. And it was obvious he cared about the environment. She'd hardly be marrying the devil incarnate.

He'd made it clear that the marriage would be in name only. There was no expectation of a relationship. He'd been at pains to spell out their living arrangements.

She let out an involuntary sigh.

Time to get over her crush.

This was a *strictly* business proposal.

Her fingers hovered over her phone as she considered her reply.

If she didn't go through with this, then the alternative lay in front of her like a stark truth.

She was nearly thirty, living alone in a cramped one bed flat dating losers. Meeting someone, getting married, having kids even; it was all highly unlikely any time soon.

And anyway; Jean-Paul, the one man she'd given her heart to, was proof enough for her that falling in love only meant pain. She was determined never to pick the pieces of herself off the floor like that again.

Enough self-pity. She was in a great place right now and she was really happy being single. As a chef, she was on top of her game. And she'd said that she was ready for a new career challenge.

What more could she ask for than her very own restaurant?

This business proposal could work. Why the heck not?

To give Gareth credit, it was a damn fine idea.

They could both still act like they were single and they could meet the terms of the will.

Plus, they could get divorced at any point with a clear carve-up of the assets. It was future-proofed.

And it would mean that she could live in Freshwater Bay.

She tapped out her answer in a flurry. Sending back her response before she changed her mind.

Gareth had heard nothing all day.

He knew she was driving back to London and so hadn't worried too much at first.

But, you'd think that when a man asks a woman to marry him in the morning, he might get an answer by teatime at least?

It was after ten o'clock at night when his phone finally beeped.

'With regards to your strictly business proposal and the terms,

I'm in.

Yes, Gareth, I will marry you.

Beth'

Holy shit! She said yes.

He hadn't expected that.

The longer he'd waited, he'd been certain that if he had a response at all it would be a no.

His heart pounded.

It was probably the idea of marriage, he rationalised. It still put the fear of God in him, after the last time. He hoped she understood exactly what the terms were.

His life was about to change.

Thank you, Uncle Evan.

With a bit of luck, he could now get things rolling on his eco-chalets. His mind was spinning with the next steps. Planning proposals, submission of drawings, meeting with the bank, getting the boathouse finished, booking the registry office...

This would now mean two loveless marriages. Precisely what he'd said he didn't want.

His parents wouldn't be impressed, either. Ellen and David had made their feelings clear when he told them about the first divorce.

They accepted that Gareth's relationship with Chantelle was broken. But even when he'd spelled it out for them, told them everything she'd done, they still argued that their vows had been taken before God. When a couple disagreed about stuff they'd told him, you had to communicate. Work through it together.

Easy for them to preach. They'd loved each other when they got married. Hand on heart, he never loved Chantelle. In fact, he'd never loved anyone. Not in that all-consuming way that Madog had loved Caitlin.

For him, relationships were a disaster and this was the best option for him.

He typed back.

'Great. Call you tomorrow evening, around 9pm?'

Beth didn't pick up the reply straight away. She was dancing on the settee, whooping loudly, waving cushions in the air.

She was going to be the proud owner and Head Chef of Le Gallois in the most beautiful place in Wales. She was going to live by the sea!

She searched her bag for the restaurant keys and held them

lovingly in her hand. Funny how she hadn't quite got around to posting them back to the solicitors.

She laughed out loud to herself like a madwoman.

Thank you, Evan! Thank you, Mr Poker Up Your Arse!

Her life was about to change forever.

She had so much to do. She'd need to hand in her notice at work. Tell her landlord she was leaving. Pack up her things for the move. There was the refurbishment, then menus, costings, suppliers, breweries, wine merchants... and... what on earth she was going to wear to the registry office? What was the sham bride dress code these days?

She couldn't do this alone. She so needed Alys and Jo.

Alys would be gushing and Jo would be judging. Jo had very strong views and she didn't fancy arguing the toss with her over this one.

So what, that she was trading in love and children for her career?

It sounded awful when she viewed it like that. But, this was a much better route for her.

And look at her now? She couldn't be happier with her choice.

She read through the texts again.

She had a new message from Gareth arranging a call for the following evening.

Bollocks!

She stopped in her tracks.

She scrolled through the message chain again.

He did write that.

He owned the boathouse.

She cast her mind back to her swim. The place was empty. His pickup truck wasn't there. But then, she thought she'd seen a movement at the window.

What if he'd seen her swimming naked?

She swallowed her utter embarrassment with a large gulp of hot chocolate.

CHAPTER 11

---------*---------

G areth video-called the next evening.
He'd not wasted any time getting things moving. Once he'd made a decision, Beth realised, Gareth was determined to make it happen. And she was happy to be swept along by his enthusiasm.

He paused and stared gravely at her, directly into the camera. Even over video link, he made her a little flustered.

"Beth, are you sure you want to go through with this?"

His face filled the screen. Those intense eyes of his were looking directly at her, doing things he had no idea about to her.

If she didn't lighten things up, she'd never be able to go through with this wedding. She'd fancy him too much.

It was time to have some fun at his expense.

Make him squirm for once.

"Actually, Gareth. I've been mulling it over a lot in my mind since yesterday."

She drew a breath and did an overly long, talent show pause.

His face clouded over and she noticed for the first time, the colour of his eyes. They were an unusual blue-grey. Like slate in the rain.

"Nah! I'm only messin' with ya."

She gave him a broad, cheesy grin and the clouds lifted from Gareth's face.

"Your proposal's the best thing that's happened to me in, well...

forever."

She heard him exhale and it dawned on her what she'd said.

"What I mean is, it's not every day you get handed your dream on a plate."

It was the first smile she'd seen from him in the call. It disappeared too quickly though, like Welsh winter sunshine.

Gareth was soon all business again. He wanted to make that clear too, from the outset.

He'd set the call up like a meeting.

Agenda Item Number One: Marriage.

He'd found out all the details, they had to give notice of intention to marry, and he'd made a few calls already to registry offices looking for a date in the next few weeks.

"Places are booked up months in advance, Beth. Apparently, spring and summer are their busiest times."

"That's odd."

He gave her an admonishing look. Her sarcasm wasn't being appreciated.

She smiled angelically into the screen.

Did his stony face crack for a second there?

No. It was back to business.

Gareth had a list of actions for her.

"If you get the documents and fees to them, they have a cancellation in May, mid-week. I've provisionally booked it. Is that acceptable to you?"

He found the name and address of the registry office for her. It was in the next borough.

"That would be most acceptable, Mr Morgan. I will pop it into my calendar right away."

He gave her a stern look and she found herself raising her chin in defiance.

He ran his fingers through his hair and leaned back a little from the screen.

"Sorry, Beth. I don't want to push you. But I can't see the point of hanging about."

Beth's shoulders slumped. She'd seen a chink in his armour but he was still being very goal-focussed.

"Me neither. May's perfect."

It would give them a few weeks to sort things out, but not too long to wait to get it over and done with.

"Send me through your bank details and I'll transfer the fees to you."

Beth bristled.

"No way are you paying for it all, Gareth."

"I'm old fashioned, that way."

"This isn't a date. We're business partners. So it's fifty-fifty with our joint costs, okay?"

She sniggered.

"It may even be tax-deductible."

"If you're sure?"

"I am."

With their immediate plans settled, Gareth seemed to relax a little. She liked that, and she kept him on the call, trying to draw him into conversation. It was a little stilted at first but she chipped away, bantering lightly with him, breaking him down bit by bit.

He told her about Madog.

She could tell that Gareth was surprised about how much Beth knew already about Caitlin's death and the baby. But it did help him open up.

"Madog said Jake was up all night. Really grizzly. He thinks he's having his first tooth. Madog was like a zombie this morning. He mixed up the bottles and nearly fed Jake the lambs' milk."

In turn, Beth talked to him about Alys and Jo. About going out in London, and how they were both going to be shocked when they heard about her inheritance.

Mr Pokerface was much more friendly and at ease now. Although she still wasn't quite sure what was going on behind those flinty eyes and that impassive chiselled face.

"We're all going out on Saturday night for a few drinks. I hardly ever get a Saturday off, so I'm looking forward to it."

"Sounds fun."

"Are you going to tell them?"

She studied his face. Was he testing her?

"Only about the restaurant."

"Yes. I think that's wise."

"I'll keep the registry office secret between us."

She couldn't for some reason bring herself to call it a wedding or a marriage. He seemed to be avoiding those words too.

"That's what we agreed. It's for the best, Beth. This way no one gets hurt."

The logic of his argument washed away her excitement.

"You're right. They're my best mates but I don't want them judging me about this business arrangement."

Gareth went quiet. He was still there but seemed unsure of what to say.

After a few seconds, he spoke.

"I get how hard it is not to tell them, Beth. Same for me with my parents. They're very traditional. This deal will only cause them more pain. Especially when they find out I've divorced again."

He was still raw about his divorce. She got that. And she'd met his parents. Seen the community. But his choice of phrasing screamed in her ears.

'When they find out I've divorced again'

Whatever secret fantasies she might be harbouring, she needed to wise up. He had every intention of divorcing her as soon as he legally could.

She switched tack.

"I've got a confession to make."

He looked at her quirkily.

She needed to forget the crush she had and move them into the friend zone. Fast.

"So... I may have trolled your Facebook profile last night... You need to seriously sort it out, pal. If I was a fraudster, I have your date and place of birth, your full name and a whole heap of other personal stuff."

"You do?"

"Uh-huh."

He looked concerned. It was working.

"Like what?"

"Like how great you look dressed as a banana."

She laughed at his surprised face. He was definitely thawing. He let out a deep breath.

"*Aaahhh*, the Banana Man costume."

"Yes, my friend. That kind of photographic material is part of your indelible digital footprint. It'll be there with you in cyber-space forever."

Beth couldn't help it. She'd been curious about Gareth's past. She didn't tell him she'd seen it, but there in the middle of his tagged photos of lads' nights out and partying holiday shots, was a picture of him with his arm around a glamorous woman with long, platinum blonde hair. She knew at once that this was his ex-wife.

Chantelle was immaculately dressed in a tight designer red dress. On her hand was a large diamond rock of an engagement ring, which she casually displayed in her pose for the camera.

Beth's heart had sunk.

The photos had given her the shake and wake she needed. She had no illusions as to why Gareth was so keen to keep this business proposal a secret.

A five foot two chef, who spent most of her time in a hot kitchen smelling of onions and garlic. She was hardly up there with his usual footballer's wife standards.

Gareth's face had finally melted. Grinning at her, for the first time Beth saw his face light up. He looked younger and disturbingly handsome.

"You stalking me, chef?"

"Well, yes okay, maybe a little... but only when you dress up as a piece of fruit."

"Whatever peels your banana, babe."

Beth rolled her eyes at him.

"Don't flatter yourself, pal."

CHAPTER 12

----------*----------

O n Saturday evening, she met up with Alys and Jo and broke the news of her inheritance to them as they sat drinking happy hour cocktails at a busy bar by the river.

As agreed, she kept the terms of the inheritance and that she was getting married a secret. It rankled her. And she hoped they'd forgive her. They'd not be her bridesmaids. Not this time around, anyway.

When they heard about the restaurant they whooped too.

"Bloody Hell, Beth! " Jo said, after ordering more cocktails. "And it's on the seafront, you say? How much is that worth?"

"I dunno. It doesn't matter 'cos I'm not selling it. I'd never do that to Evan."

Alys screwed her nose.

"And he never even gave me his recipe for pain couronne. You're a jammy beggar, Beth. You know that."

Beth gave her a conciliatory smile.

"I'd rather have Evan back with us again."

Jo wobbled on her barstool as the drinks arrived at their high table.

"That was a close one. One Long Sloe Screw too many."

Alys giggled.

"I've had four Screaming Orgasms. I've broken my record."

"Which was?"

She stuck up three fingers.

Beth looked at her impressively.

"Where've I been going wrong all my life?"

Jo chipped in.

"'It's cos you keep swiping losers on Tinder."

She didn't disagree.

She sucked deeply on her straw. Her Pop My Cherry cocktail was going down far too quickly.

"I love going out with you two stars. I'm going to miss you guys so much."

They were her world in London.

"You'd better come visit me."

Alys and Jo hugged her.

"You bet."

She'd been living in London for nine years.

Talking to Gareth every night, she felt that she was starting to connect with Freshwater Bay and the people there. Still, it wasn't quite a reality yet. And being in a small community after living so long in a large city was going to be a culture shock.

Gareth was beginning to open up. He was relaxed with her now and she saw that stunning smile of his more often.

Trouble was, they were now strictly in the friend zone, bantering with each other like besties.

It was probably just as well. It would be super-awkward for them to be in this business partnership with her drooling over him.

"I wanna dance!"

Jo and Alys pulled faces at each other.

"Beth, you always wanna dance."

It was true. She always pestered them to go to a club after they went out for drinks. She'd danced as a kid in competitions. For Beth, the dance floor was her happy place. Where she could get lost in the beat.

Jo yawned.

"Looks like it'll be another late one, then."

They drank up and headed to their favourite place. Arms

around each other, swaying a little as they went.

"I still can't believe you're leaving us, hun. What we going to do without ya?" Alys said sadly.

"Why on earth d'ya wanna go to the middle of nowhere, anyway?" Jo grumbled. "Sheep and cow shit everywhere. No shops, no phone signal, dodgy wifi. Urgh!"

"Oi!"

"Sorry Alys, I forgot you're Welsh. It's 'cos you sound like a Scouser," Jo teased.

Alys gave her a mock huff and they both hugged Beth tightly.

Jo pulled away abruptly.

"Bet you, she's got a bloke there."

She stared Beth in the eye and pointed at her nose.

"I'm a bloody good journalist, Missy. And I'm sniffing a story."

"She's been snapchatting someone all night."

Now Alys was dobbing her in too.

"Have you had a holiday fling with some Welsh lad?"

"No! Oh my God, you two! Are you saying I copped off at a funeral?"

Jo sniggered.

"The lady doth protest too much, methinks."

"No! I do not protesteth too muchos! Anyways, I'm sworn off men after Dave. I've even deleted Tinder. See."

Beth started showing them her phone screen.

"Yeah, yeah. Whatever... Who's this notification from, then?"

Beth coloured up. There was a new message from Gareth.

"Uh... no one. He's an architect. He's helping me with the restaurant, that's all."

The girls burst into giggles.

"What!" Beth exclaimed, exasperated.

Jo rolled her eyes in triumphant.

"Told you I was good."

The girls danced themselves sober.

Exhausted and sick of sleazebags trying to hit on them, they left as dawn was breaking. Escaping out onto the shabby litter-strewn London street, they hailed a taxi to take them home.

CHAPTER 13

----------*---------

Evening was becoming Gareth's favourite time. Sometimes they talked into the small hours, especially if Beth was working an evening shift.

They'd settled the business arrangements, but if this was going to work they needed to be friends.

She was easy to talk to, so full of life. She made him laugh.

"How'd it go at work today?" she asked him as her face filled the screen of his laptop.

"Fine. It's been hot. Oh, and the kitchen carcasses and doors came today."

He combed his fingers through his hair.

"I'm hoping to be moved in before you get here. I'm sick of this boat."

It was late, way after eleven, and they were both drinking red wine as they chatted.

Beth was lying on her bed, her golden hair billowing down her shoulders onto her tight, white vest top which showed more than she realised.

Gareth wasn't for telling her. He was secretly enjoying the camera view.

The deal was purely business but that didn't mean he couldn't look, right? He needed something to dream about, and the curves of her breasts would do for a start.

Beth yawned.

"I've been on the charcoal grill cooking ribeye all day."

She grabbed a hunk of her golden curls and sniffed them.

"I've had a bath but I still smell of burnt cow."

Gareth chuckled.

"All set for the move?"

"Marcel offered me more money to stay. He thought I'd been headhunted by the Michelin starred Italian down the road."

Gareth hoped she'd refused.

Beth took a sip of her wine.

"Don't go all stony-faced on me. I said no."

Gareth couldn't help but smirk. She kept saying he'd a stern look about him. He couldn't see it himself.

"When I told Marcel about Le Gallois, he hugged me. He's given me details of his specialist food suppliers and wine merchant. He even offered to help out, which was sweet of him. Now I just need a brewery."

"I'm sending you Harry Hops' details. He's got a micro-brewery in town. Hold on…"

Gareth checked his contacts and sent her a text. He heard it ping on Beth's phone.

"Ah, thanks. That's great. Crafted beers'd be perfect for the restaurant."

She grinned.

"Harry Hops? A brewer? Is that for real?"

"Yeah, well, it's Wales. Too many Joneses and Davieses, so our names are like what we do, or where we live. I dunno it kinda sticks."

Beth flicked her hair out of her face.

"So you're like … Bob the Builder?"

"Not quite. I'm Gareth Cae Môr. That's the farm name. Means fields by the sea."

"What'll they call me, I wonder?"

She seemed a little tense.

"All set for *the big day?*"

Neither of them wanted to call it what it was. Or wasn't.

"I had an email from the registry office," Beth confirmed. "All good to go. We're booked in for twelve o'clock."

Gareth was tentative. How was she going to take this? Chantelle would have had a meltdown.

"I've got a problem."

Beth looked at him playfully on the screen.

"Don't tell me. You're still married?"

"Ha, ha. Very funny... No. It's the chalet development. The planners want an on-site meeting at eleven the day after."

He tried to gauge her reaction. She was still smiling.

He carried on.

"It's standard stuff. But if I don't handle it properly it could mess up the planning permission. I'll have to get the five o'clock train back."

They had planned to go out in London after the registry office. He was going to crash on the sofa at hers and then help her with the move the following day.

But what choice did he have?

"Beth, I'm sorry."

She took another sip of wine.

"And there I was, hoping you'd be riding off with me into the sunset on a white stallion."

She flicked her hair dramatically.

"Instead, I'm being dumped. And not even for another lover."

His eyes widened at her cheeky dig.

"You're dumping me for a bloomin' planning meeting."

Gareth took a gulp of wine. It was a shitty thing to do. Marry her, then leave her.

"Hey, Gareth. It's only a piece of paper. It's not a real wedding. Don't sweat."

He breathed a little more easily.

"Seriously, Gareth. There's no question about it, you've *got* to be there. Don't worry, I'll hire a removals company."

He loved the way she dealt with problems head-on. She was going to be awesome running the restaurant.

"No need. I've sorted it. Vinnie the Van's coming. It's my bad."

She grinned.

"Don't tell me. Delivery driver?"

"No, he's got an ice cream van in the summer."

"Smart arse... Hold on. He's not coming in that is he?"

"You'll have to wait and see."

Gareth still felt bad. Weddings were a big deal for chicks.

Chantelle had been the original Bridezilla. She'd been a maniac about the details.

Beth and Chantelle were chalk and cheese, thank God. But, was this all a front? Would she wind up being bitter and twisted about it?

He began to fish.

"I'm sorry Beth, that this isn't how you planned, you know, your big day."

A pause.

"Leave it out, will ya. News flash, buddy. You're not breaking my heart. And you're not my Prince Charming. This is a business deal. End of."

He'd been put in his place. He should be relieved at what she'd said.

He took another drink of wine.

"What's happened? I thought you were my stalker?"

"Listen, Banana Boy. If you think I'm going to swoon in your arms and beg you to seduce me as soon we're hitched, forget it, pal. The only thing that gets me turned on is the sight of a stainless-steel range cooker and a certain hundred cover restaurant."

"I'll remember that."

"But...when I *do* turn up at the town hall in my horse-drawn carriage wearing my humongous white, bridal meringue with ten bridesmaids in tow, you'd better not start getting all dewy-eyed on me. I don't want none of that soppy, romantic shit from you, okay?"

"Trust me, sweetheart, if I catch sight of ten bridesmaids and a big white dress, I'll be sprinting from there faster than Usain Bolt."

They laughed.

By now they were both quite drunk and he was feeling a little reckless.

"Beth?"

"Hmm?"

"You're so easy to talk to, you know that. I could never've talked to Chantelle like this. To be honest, I used to dread going home. Walking through the door, not knowing what bomb she was going to drop on me next."

He told her everything. He couldn't stop. The credit card bills she racked up. His unhappiness. Her affair with his best mate. His relief when it was over.

"But you gave up everything? Moved away. Are you happy being a builder? You could have a shit-hot job as an architect if you lived here in London?"

"True. But I love Freshwater Bay. And being a builder's made me a better architect. Plus, it keeps me in good shape."

"Certainly does."

Beth choked on her wine.

"Sorry. Drink went down the wrong way."

"It's so good to be single again," Gareth added.

"What about sex?"

He was surprised by her directness.

"Uhh.. sex? Well, since you ask. All I want is uncomplicated. No emotional shit, no baggage, no relationships."

He didn't know why he was being so honest. But she had asked.

"Ah, you haven't met the right girl, that's all. You will. One day." She sounded mushy.

"No. I don't believe in all that romantic crap. That's why I'm marrying you."

He heard Beth's sharp intake of breath.

"Same here."

She'd gone quiet.

"Hey, I'm sorry. That came out wrong."

"It's alright. You got burned by Chantelle. I understand where you're coming from. I got burned too."

"When?

"It's the reason I agreed to go through with this. I couldn't marry someone who was actually husband material."

Ouch. He'd upset her.

"Tell me about it."

She sniffed.

"Beth."

"I never talk about it."

"You can tell me."

She sighed.

"Alright... I was working in a restaurant in Paris. There was this French chef called Jean-Paul. I was nineteen and I was completely smitten. I moved in with him."

Propping herself up on her elbow, she talked into the camera.

"Then, things changed pretty fast. He stopped me going out with my friends. Started telling me what to wear, even made me change my hair. Next thing, he was saying I was putting on weight. Every little thing, he picked at. I could never do right from wrong."

Gareth's mouth twitched. The guy sounded like a right controlling bastard.

"He was my first proper boyfriend and he was older than me. I thought it was how relationships were. I tried hard to please him, but it was never enough."

She shifted nervously.

"After a few months, I fell pregnant. He was shouting at me a lot by then and I was scared of how he'd react, so I kept it quiet. Then, one Sunday morning I told him."

"What did he do?"

"When I was in the shower he told me through the door that he was going out to get some coffee and croissants. He never came back. He quit his job the same day and left Paris."

Gareth couldn't speak. His teeth were gritted and his fists were screwed tightly into a ball out of camera shot. Nineteen, alone in Paris. And pregnant.

"I was so scared and confused, Gareth, I tried to block it out. I did double shifts, worked from the morning until late at night. I was hauling a sack of spuds up from the cellar when I had a pain.

The doctor said the miscarriage could have been caused by anything. Listeriosis, heavy lifting, stress. I left Paris after that. I... I wanted to go home. See my mum."

Gareth felt a sharp pang.

"I wish I could give you a hug."

She looked at the screen.

"Thanks, mate."

She took a sip of wine.

"Mum was there when I got off the bus. I didn't recognise her. I'd no idea she was sick. I hugged and hugged her and then we went home. I never spoke about Paris. She'd hidden her illness from me. She died six months after."

Her eyes darted up at Gareth, they were teary.

"I'm glad I was there for her at the end."

She stared absently beyond the screen.

"Beth, I'm sorry."

"Me too."

His issues paled into insignificance compared with what she'd had to endure. All alone in a different country with no family to help her.

"So. Yeah. That's my relationships, baggage and emotional shit. All wrapped up for ya, right there."

He felt an overwhelming wave of tenderness towards her.

He longed to be with her. To hold her tight.

She pouted at him, pointing at her head.

"It's taken me a good few years to grow this mop back."

He smiled back at her.

"Don't listen to that French tosser, you have really, really great hair."

She flicked it flirtily.

"And, like you, pal..."

She took a gulp of wine.

"I've not done long term relationships since."

"You mean, you've not had a boyfriend in ten years?"

"No! 'Course I've dated. I meet guys in clubs and stuff."

He'd definitely have hooked up with her if he'd met her in a bar.

"But, there's been no one I've wanted to be with long term."

"Good."

It slipped out, and he cleared his throat.

"What I mean is, you and me, Beth. We're both on the same page."

"Plus, " she grinned at him, "The men I meet, they always turn out to be total goons."

What did that say about him?

"Everyone always teases me about it actually; including your Uncle Evan. I'm telling you all this. You're like Oprah! I'm totally over Jean-Paul, by the way. But it was a motivation for me agreeing... I get it though, if you want to change your mind?"

She was fidgeting now, staring nervously at the screen.

"I'm so sorry, Gareth. I'm gonna go. I've had too much wine."

Beth moved to end the call.

"Wait up, Beth. Please."

His voice came out a little choked.

"Thanks for sharing your emotional shit and baggage with me. But you don't get out of our agreement that easily, my friend."

She looked at him curiously.

"I'm not going anywhere. If you pull out of this partnership, there'll be no fancy eco-chalets for me. So, I'm being totally selfish here when I say, we're in this together."

She looked relieved.

"Thanks, Gareth."

She smirked.

"You know, I thought you were so up yourself when we first met."

"You did?"

Chantelle had flung that at him too.

"Yeah. I used to call you Mr Poker Up Your Arse."

He laughed out loud.

"I deserved it too, if I remember right."

"You're a big softie really."

His heart suddenly hardened.

Was she getting too attached? For her sake, he had to make it clear.

"Beth, I hope you'll meet someone who treats you like you deserve to be treated. You know that it can't be me, right?"

He immediately regretted it. His words had poured out like a firewall, protecting himself.

She was silent for a second. Then, she let out a derisive laugh, but he could see the hurt in her eyes.

"Don't worry, Gareth. I'll marry you but I'll never be your girlfriend. Even if you beg me. This is all about the restaurant and nothing else."

CHAPTER 14

----------*----------

Beth didn't know where the six weeks since her return to London had gone. Gareth had moved into the boathouse and she'd been working hard on her restaurant plans.

Marcel agreed with her, it needed to be mid-range and family-oriented if it was going to be financially viable. It couldn't be Michelin star quality, but the trick was to surprise and delight. Create drama. She'd learned a trick or two in her time and she couldn't wait to get started.

She was now turning her attention to branding and design. It was an important part of any restaurant, but she was no expert.

Gareth had suggested Ariana. Beth agreed. She'd called her and had set up a meeting. She'd also phoned Harry Hops. He was a real character. A Kiwi. They'd chatted for ages about his micro-brewery business.

With the first appointments in her diary and now that *the big day* had arrived, this arrangement was fast becoming a reality. She couldn't quite believe that tomorrow she'd be in Freshwater Bay.

Both of them were crystal clear about the rules of engagement. She'd be lying if she said his words hadn't stung her. But she was glad she'd managed to slap him down too. It was going to be so much easier moving to somewhere new with a friend there to talk to and rely on.

And whenever her traitorous eyes strayed to those muscular

shoulders of his. Or when she started wondering what it would be like to have those strong arms around her, her head buried in his broad chest, she reminded herself of Chantelle's photo.

She'd seen the kind of women Gareth went for, and there was no way she could match up to such levels of perfection.

Within the confines of their friendship, a little flirting appeared to be fine, as was their friendly banter. That was as far as it went.

But of all Beth's dilemmas over the past six weeks, the thing she'd agonised most over, was what to wear. And what made it even worse, was that she couldn't confide in anyone. Jo would have been brilliant at helping her. But she was totally on her own in this whole thing.

And she missed her mum.

At least the day would be over quickly. He'd be gone on the five o'clock train.

She'd been sorely tempted to wear the grandest wedding dress she could find on eBay as a joke. His face would've been a picture.

In the end, she didn't.

She plumped for playing it casual.

But, that didn't mean a girl couldn't make an effort to look her best, right?

Even if he only ever saw her again in stained chef whites, at least he would remember that she did once, for one day, look pretty.

She'd ordered and returned packages and packages of clothing until, at last she found the one. It was a navy summer dress. There was no way she was marrying in white.

Its spaghetti shoulder straps held up a wrapped v-necked bodice. The top part of the dress fitted tightly, creating a defined waist that favoured her curves. The skirt part of the dress flowed loosely down. In the front, there was slit giving a flash of leg.

It was sexy but also the kind of summery going out dress that she'd wear to a fancy restaurant. It didn't smack of trying too hard, she hoped.

She'd been at the hairdresser first thing and her hair was in a half updo falling over her shoulders in long, styled curls.

She checked herself in the mirror; one of the few things not packed away in a cardboard box.

She was pleased. It had taken a lot of effort, but she was satisfied with the result.

She'd been quite cool about everything throughout the morning. But sitting alone in the back of the cab on the way to the town hall, it suddenly smacked into her like a wave.

This was no joke. She was about to marry a stranger. A man she'd met only once before.

She hoped he was going to be there. What if he'd changed his mind?

A thousand worries began to creep into her head and she tried to bat each one away.

There'd been nothing to indicate that he was wavering. The wedding was his idea in the first place. And he was definitely on his way there because he'd called her from Cardiff the night before and they'd chatted for over an hour. He was staying with his brother Owen so he could get an early train.

The taxi neared the junction to turn onto the high street. The town hall was a hundred metres from there.

Then, as they stopped at the traffic lights, she caught sight of him.

He was by the town hall steps, pacing and scanning the stream of traffic. And he had flowers in his hand.

She swallowed a hard lump in her throat. This was happening.

The taxi drew closer and she could see him properly now.

He looked handsome. And so serious; that granite expression was fixed on his face again. She hoped he wouldn't be too disappointed when he saw her.

She noted his choice of clothes. An open-necked cornflower blue shirt and a well-cut navy suit. No tie. He was playing it casual too.

They pulled up by the registry office and she paid the fare.

Gareth came over to open the cab door.

"For you."

He handed her a posy of forget-me-nots. A spray of tiny, delicate turquoise flowers. The colour of the sea.

They matched his shirt and her dress perfectly. It was a complete coincidence, but a good omen, nevertheless.

It was not often that Gareth was lost for words. But in that moment Beth took every single one of them from his head.

She was a sight to behold.

Her hair dropped around her delicate shoulders in golden tresses and her dress was so elegant and so damn sexy, plunging towards her breasts but giving nothing away. And as she moved, it revealed a hint of those wonderful, slender legs.

He needed to pull himself together. Quickly.

Squash those forbidden impulses that were coursing through every part of him and act like they were mates.

"Looking good today, Miss Barnes. You scrub up well for a chef who usually smells of onions and burnt cow."

"Not so bad yourself, Mr Morgan," she retaliated right back at him. "Nice to see you in a suit for once. Getting hitched, are we? Or are you up in court again?"

Typical Beth.

She smiled at him.

"Shall we?"

"Beth, you look absolutely stunning, by the way," he whispered into her ear as they walked up the steps.

Nailed it.

They were directed towards a waiting room where they sat down together. His jaw became fixed and she felt the tension in his hand as he gripped hers.

It felt surreal. After spending so long talking with him online, Gareth was now sitting beside her, in the flesh.

He squeezed her hand.

Beth gasped.

"Rings!"

Her throat was dry.

How could she have forgotten that? Maybe, because up until this point, she'd refused to accept this event was a real wedding.

"Covered."

Reaching into his jacket pocket he produced an antique gold wedding ring and a velvet pouch.

"That's not your old one, from your last..."

"No."

Beth was relieved. She was all for being thrifty but there were limits.

"It's Evan's ring. It came in a box from the solicitors. It felt like the right thing to do."

"That's lovely. It's like he's here with us today. I wonder what he'd make of this, though?"

"I think he'd be pleased."

He studied the ring.

"He'd be pleased we worked it out. Got what we both wanted."

She didn't disagree. She pictured him chuckling at them both sitting there. Two failures in love.

It was ironic. Evan said he'd fix her up with a man. He kind of had. Bet he never would have anticipated this.

She pointed to the small velvet pouch in Gareth's hand.

"Is that my ring?"

"You'll see."

"Tease."

They sat in silence for a while, watching the clock tick. Waiting for their slot. He was nervous too.

He cleared his throat.

"No second thoughts?"

Beth looked at the clock. Five minutes to go.

"We don't have to go through with this, Beth, if you don't want to."

"No. I want to. I was thinking about what my mum would say,

that's all."

Tracing light circles on the back of her hand with his thumb, he gave her a tender smile.

"It must be hard not having her around."

"Yes. It is."

She exhaled deeply.

"Gareth; let's do this. This partnership is going to change our lives."

"Yes, it is."

The registrar came through to tell them that they were ready. Gareth stood up.

Facing her, he gazed at her questioningly.

She nodded and rose to stand by his side.

His fingers wove tightly into hers as they followed the official to the front of the empty ceremony room.

They both stood facing each other. Ready to take their vows. The registrar cut in.

"Witnesses? Who are acting as your witnesses, please?"

Gareth looked at her blankly and Beth pulled a face. They'd both forgotten about that.

Ten minutes later, the registrar had roped in an elderly couple who'd come in to query their council tax bill.

Beth flinched as they said that they'd be only too pleased to help such a nice young couple who were so obviously in love.

For the second time, they faced each other. This time, with an audience of two.

And the wedding began.

On direction from the registrar, Gareth produced the rings from his pocket. The ring he'd chosen for her slipped out of the velvet pouch into Gareth's palm.

Beth let out a gasp.

It was the same ring. She was sure of it. The tree of life ring that she'd tried on at Ariana's studio. It was so beautiful with its delicate rose gold filigree and those trinity shaped leaves; she'd know it anywhere.

But Ariana had said the ring was a Celtic love ring? It wasn't right accepting this, knowing that the marriage was, well, what it was. A marriage of convenience.

Her pulse raced even harder.

Her hands became clammy. The room was a blur. She was in a tailspin, desperately trying not to overthink it, but was this ring a sign that what they were doing was wrong?

Should she call it all off? Stop the whole thing now?

The registrar had paused.

She felt like she was about to have a panic attack. She couldn't breathe.

She heard Gareth speaking.

"Just a second, please."

His eyes were fixed on Beth.

"Beth?" he whispered under his breath. "Everything alright?"

She heard his voice.

She felt his fingers gently brushing her cheek.

She turned her eyes to his, losing herself for a moment in them. What she had with Gareth, it didn't feel like they were doing anything wrong.

She focussed on breathing out calmly.

Remember the restaurant. This is what Evan wanted.

She managed a weak smile.

"I'm fine now," she mouthed to Gareth.

She tried to smile more confidently at the registrar.

"I just got a little overwhelmed," she said quietly to him. "Wedding day nerves. Please carry on."

She heard Gareth exhaling deeply.

He placed the ring on her finger. It fitted perfectly; and she knew at once, as it slipped on, that this was indeed the ring she'd tried on before.

This time though, it felt good when she wore it and that steadied her too.

She repeated her vows perfectly. And with Evan's ring sliding onto his finger, Gareth did likewise.

"I now pronounce you husband and wife."

It was done.

"You may kiss the bride."

They faced each other a little uncertainly. This hadn't been in the script she'd planned in her head. This was a registry office, not a church. But if they didn't kiss, well then, there might be suspicions raised about their marriage and she didn't want that either.

She gazed up at him searchingly.

Leaning in towards her, Gareth sought her permission and she nodded breathlessly.

His face lowered towards hers, and then, she felt the lightest feathery brush of his lips on hers.

The electricity crackling between them was almost too much for her to bear. He pressed a little more and lingered as she kissed him back. Cautiously at first, and then opening for him to deepen the kiss. His tongue grazing against her bottom lip in tentative exploration when neither of them pulled away.

His hand gently brushed her cheek and he ended it.

Her heart pounded as their lips drew apart. But she couldn't draw her eyes away, and neither could he. And they burned with the same thrillingly intense desire that she felt too.

Business arrangement?

She was so screwed.

CHAPTER 15

----------*---------

With the ceremony over, Mr and Mrs Morgan wandered out of the town hall into the May sunshine. Beth gave her lovely spray of forget-me-nots to a little girl who was with her mother waiting for a bus.

Gareth was torn. All he could think about was how she'd tasted when he kissed her. She was so responsive to him. He was sure that she wanted him too.

Should he take her in his arms and kiss her? Right here, right now. Go back to hers and forget about the meeting tomorrow. He wanted her so badly. This business arrangement business was never going to work.

And, Jees! That dress. More than anything, he wanted to explore the curves wrapped up beneath it. Run his hands up those silky legs that kept sneaking into view. She had no idea how stunningly beautiful she was.

Or what she was doing to him.

No, this was not how today was meant to go at all.

The one woman who he'd wanted from the moment he'd clapped eyes on her, he could never have. In fact, he couldn't ever remember wanting anyone else as much as this.

And now they were man and wife.

Great. Why had he told her he was off-limits?

And she'd made it abundantly clear that she'd never get with him, either. Even if he begged.

He considered it some more.

If begging would help, he'd gladly do it.

This mess, it was all his doing. He was doomed.

He strolled in silence with her through the park. Both of them holding onto each other by the hand. Neither of them able to figure out what to do next.

Surely, she felt that charge between them too?

A pub.

That's what they needed right now, he decided. A drink, some food, a matey chat till four, and then the train home at five. Back to safety.

He broke the silence.

"Let's get a drink, Mrs Morgan."

"Great idea, Mr Morgan."

She sounded relieved. So was he.

She'd gone very quiet. And after her panic in the ceremony, he hoped that she wasn't regretting it already.

They chose a fashionable looking place that was once an old meeting hall and made their way to the large mahogany mirrored bar.

It was lined with easily over a hundred bottles of gin, and manned by a young hipster barman in a tight black T-shirt with a long beard and tattoo sleeves.

"Two Tanqueray and tonics please."

Beth looked quizzically at Gareth. They'd both heard the unmistakable sound of a quartet orchestra playing a waltz in the large hall next door to the bar.

The barman gestured with his head towards the music.

"Tea dance. It's a new thing. Trying to pull in the afternoon golden oldies. Tea dance today, bongo bingo tonight."

"Bongo bingo?"

Beth laughed at Gareth's confused face.

"Yeah, it's like bingo and clubbing put together. Don't worry about it."

How long had he been in Freshwater Bay? He was definitely feeling like a country bumpkin now.

Beth's ears had pricked up when she heard about the tea dance.

"Wanna take a peek?" she suggested.

He was about to play with fire, but he couldn't stop himself. He wanted to feel her in his arms.

He leaned in towards her.

"No problem. But how 'bout we make it more interesting? What about a dance dare?"

"Only if I get to dare you back too," she bargained. "If I do it, I can dare you anything, right? All dares allowed, no refusal?"

This could be interesting. How mean could she be? She couldn't be any worse than his brothers.

"You're on."

They moved into the hall where the tea dance was in full swing and sat sipping their gins watching retired couples waltzing sedately around the room.

This was a very odd day.

Beth excused herself to go to the bathroom.

As she turned to walk away, Gareth quickly got up before the next dance and grabbed the attention of the violinist. He explained how he'd just got married and that they'd like a first dance.

He had one dance that he could do, and he was certain that he could impress her with it.

Beth came back to the table as the foxtrot was in its last throes.

Taking her hand, Gareth motioned her to join him on the floor.

"I dare you to dance the next one with me."

They waited at the side until the dance ended and then he led her to the middle of the dance floor as the other couples sat down.

Beth smirked smugly and he smiled back at her.

She had no idea he could dance a tango and he wasn't about to tell her.

"I hope I don't make a fool of myself," he told her.

"Take the lead from me. And watch you don't step on my feet."

A confident response. Well, they'd soon see if she could tango.

The violinist took his cue and got ready to play.

Beth glanced dubiously at Gareth as she heard the opening bars and recognised the tango.

He could tell she was thinking that he was way out of his depth. He tried to take control.

But, taking her position she held him haughtily and sexily away, at mid-arm's length.

Gareth was impressed. It appeared that she could dance too.

Beth began to move, twisting to the side and then back to him, and closer. She tantalised him as she moved away and then turned inwards again. Teasing.

Holding her firm, he moved as she did, allowing her to spin and rotate rhythmically and playfully, off and on the beat.

Her eyes widened as she saw him dance.

He tried to lead her, but she resisted.

He tried to spin her.

Spinning around, she moved *him* to do the same.

She seemed determined to show him that she wasn't to be played with. After all, the tango was a love battle and each of them thought they held all the moves.

They swept around the floor, deftly wrapping their legs around each other. Provocatively, tauntingly, totally in sync with the rhythm of the tango.

She moved closer to him. He could feel the tension between them.

Leaning against him, she swooned gracefully, arching fully backwards, rotating her back sexily as she rose again to face him. Drawing him in and then pulling away as she stretched her leg out behind her, the slit revealing the whole length of her thigh.

He drew her possessively back towards him again, trying to ignore how his pulse was racing as she swept up close against his hard body.

Who was this woman? He never thought he'd dance the tango again. He'd certainly never danced it like this.

She challenged and goaded him as they sparred. They intertwined so intimately, his heart was pounding.

He was aroused and totally under her power as she skilfully reeled him in with those dazzlingly green, teasing eyes. And her amazing body; supple and strong, powerful yet vulnerable.

The dance was ending, and as the music stopped they came together in an embrace from Beth's final spin.

Torturing him, her lips lightly grazed his. His hooded eyes fixed intensely on hers as the electricity surged between them. Breathing heavily with the emotion of the dance, both of them wrapped up in each other under the magical powers of the tango.

As he moved his mouth onto hers, properly this time, a round of applause snapped them from the spell.

Rather embarrassed to realise that they had an audience, Gareth backed away from her and led Beth off the dance floor. Quickly. Before she pulled him into the Cha Cha Cha and he'd be busted.

Sitting side by side, speechless sipping their gin and tonics, they silently recovered their composure.

"Where d'ya learn to dance like that?" he asked.

"Err..."

She was struggling with her emotions too.

"I used to dance. As a kid."

His eyes were drawn back to hers. He was still on a precipice. It wouldn't take much for her to reel him back in.

"What? Like that?" he rasped.

"No. Never like that," she answered breathily. "You were... how did you learn to dance like that?"

"Misspent youth."

"What? Ballroom dancing with the cows?"

He grinned.

"Not far off. I did a student sabbatical in Patagonia. Don't ask me how I learned to tango or I'll have to tell you a very sorry tale. Forget Paris. I was left in a heap of heartache on a Buenos Aires dancefloor."

She knocked her shoulder into his.

"Oh please. Spare me."

"Not too shabby yourself on the dancefloor, Mrs Morgan."

"Aww thanks, *hubby*."

It was a joke, but they both fell silent for a moment as reality dawned on them.

"So," Beth began. "I did your dance dare. I personally think I exceeded your expectations."

Gareth wholeheartedly agreed.

"Okay, so now it's my turn."

She turned to face him.

What was she going to say? There were a thousand things he wanted to do, mainly to her, but he wasn't going to go there. The tango had been dangerous enough.

"Go on, what is it?" he asked, amused. "What is it you want me to do?"

She stared at him curiously.

"My dare is you've gotta swim in front of *me*, this time. In the sea. Naked."

Gareth's face cracked into a broad grin.

"I knew it," she gasped. "You were there. Hiding. You saw me."

"What can I say?"

Gareth laughed and moved his arms in a defensive cover as she mock-attacked him.

He chuckled as she laid into him.

"Best damn view I've ever had out of that window," he laughed.

She punched him hard on the arm.

It was now getting towards four o'clock. Time to move and make their way across London to Paddington station.

As they rattled along on the Tube, they both became more pensive. Taking both her hands, he stopped outside the entrance to the station and turned to face her.

"Beth, thank you for today and for going through with this."

He studied her face closely. Was this just a business deal for her? Or was he right when he felt her desire in that kiss and in the tango? He never knew that a dance could be so sexually charged.

"I don't want to leave."

She brushed that, and him off lightly.

"I'll be in Freshwater Bay tomorrow; I'll see you then."

She had her game face on now.

Surely, she felt the attraction too? It had been fizzing between them all day, and even now he felt inexplicably and magnetically drawn to her.

He gazed down into her bewitching, green eyes. And, unable to stop himself any longer, he pulled her into him.

Wrapping his arms around her delicate frame, his lips crashed into hers and a hot, passionate kiss exploded between them.

She'd been surprised at first, he could tell. But then she responded eagerly and hungrily, deepening the kiss.

The sparks that they'd felt charging between them were lightning bolts now. Beth was on fire for him. He could tell.

And he wanted her too. Badly.

Right here, right now.

In the alleyway, in a toilet; wherever. He didn't care.

Did he have to go?

They kissed and kissed.

Oblivious to the traffic on the busy road. Oblivious to the commuters hastily passing around them. Oblivious to a screeching wolf whistle and Cockney heckle of *"Gerrinmyson!"* shouted from a nearby scaffolded building.

They kissed until eventually, finally, she pulled away.

She staggered back, the heat of desire still flaming through her too.

"I better get my train," he said huskily.

She exhaled, blushing, holding her head high.

"The tango. It does that to a girl."

He gently brushed a curl of her hair off her face.

Shyly, she looked down and quickly made herself busy, searching through her bag, then producing the keys to the restaurant.

She held them out to him.

"Don't forget these. Unless Vinnie's bringing the ice-cream van he'll be in Freshwater Bay before me."

Gareth had agreed to help unload her stuff.

"We'd better take these off too."

She touched her wedding ring. Then, slowly she began to slide it off her finger.

"No."

He put his hand over hers to stop her. He didn't know why but he didn't want her to take his ring off.

"We need to, Gareth. Remember our agreement. No one's to know."

His immediate reaction was that he didn't give a stuff about the agreement, but on further consideration, she did have a point.

"How about this, then?"

He took her hand and carefully slid the ring off her left finger, swapping it onto her right hand.

She did the same with his.

He grazed her forehead wistfully with his lips as they embraced in a final goodbye.

She moved to go. And he felt split apart as she turned around to wave a final farewell.

It wasn't meant to be like this.

He texted her as he waited for his train.

'See you in Freshwater Bay, Mrs Morgan'

Perhaps she was embarrassed? Perhaps she regretted the kiss? Gareth couldn't work it out.

Whatever it was, she didn't reply.

CHAPTER 16

----------✳----------

"I can't see any problems with the environmental aspect. You've done a comprehensive impact report and your zero-carbon build ticks all the boxes. In fact, we could use your expertise in helping us with other developments."

Gareth breathed easy as the lead planning officer gave him his feedback. The meeting was going well.

They'd walked the site and everything appeared to be in order. The land was on a permitted development zone. In fact, with land values soaring, the officer said that it was a miracle that it hadn't been developed years ago.

They arrived back at the restaurant car park.

"So, what next?" Gareth asked.

"The only potential sticking point is the public response."

"Ah, yes."

"We can make our recommendations but the planning will go to a council committee. If the councillors get pressured to refuse it, then no matter how sustainable and cutting-edge it is, it's unlikely to go ahead. People can get very het up about new developments."

Gareth nodded.

"I'm a local lad. So, can I suggest we hold a public meeting?"

The planning officer considered it.

"Yes, that would help."

Gareth was sure he could pull it off. He knew enough people here. He was related to a fair few.

The planning officer sought to reassure him.

"There's not a lot they can object to. You can't see the development from the village, so any concerns will be environmental or traffic-related. Both of which you've addressed."

The planning officer sounded optimistic. But Gareth knew that planning applications were curious beasts. Unseen influencers were often at play. And anything could potentially happen.

The planning officers left and Gareth strolled back alone, over the cliff tops, across *his* fields to the development site.

The long train journey home had given Gareth plenty of time to reflect on what had happened between the two of them. Had it purely been the pent-up emotion of the wedding? Or the magic of that steamy tango?

He gazed out at the sea.

How had Beth described it here? Tranquil.

Standing there, remembering how they'd kissed, his mind was far from tranquil.

And today, he'd been restless since he'd woken up. Antsy, even. She'd be arriving later on.

He couldn't delude himself anymore, he badly wanted Beth in his bed. And in that kiss, he was certain she'd felt the same way.

Afterwards though, she'd seemed confused and embarrassed. And she still hadn't replied to his text.

It wasn't surprising. That kiss had totally messed up their arrangement. It was a stupid thing to have done.

And though she denied it, like him she was scarred by her past. The fact she hadn't been in a proper relationship for years was no coincidence. Fright and flight. He'd read about people's instinctive patterns of behaviour. Beth's was flight. She was a commitment phobe.

Who was he kidding? He was one too.

And they were way too complicated for a no-strings-attached, casual sex kinda thing. She was a woman, after all. She was bound to wind up emotional. Then there'd be the rows, the mistrust and eventually the messy break-up.

He couldn't do all of that shit again.

Plus, any split would mean dividing up the estate, the restaurant and their investments.

Their kiss suddenly made things a whole heap more complicated. And he needed simple.

Once she got here, the last thing she needed was awkwardness between them. She needed to focus on getting the restaurant going so that it could hit the summer season.

Best press reset and start again, he decided.

It would kill him, but he had to keep a lid on his desires for her. They had to stay just friends.

Vinnie was outside Beth's front door with his transit van at seven the next morning.

Half an hour later everything she owned was winging its way to West Wales. She prayed her little car would get there too.

She scanned around her empty flat, looking for anything she'd missed, giving it a final clean before she locked the door for the last time.

This was the biggest move of her life and she was super-excited about the restaurant. Even so, she hoped that she was doing the right thing.

Last night, she'd lain in bed, everything around her packed in boxes. She replayed the day over in her head. She was now Mrs Beth Morgan.

What exactly was going on between them? They'd been playing a dangerous game with that tango. And then that kiss. It had been an emotional day and they'd gotten carried away. It was a good job he hadn't stayed or who knows where they'd have wound up?

Between her sheets. There was no denying the passion they both felt for each other. She'd never been kissed like that before. Her whole body ached for him.

Instead, she'd drunk hot chocolate and read a book. So much for her wedding night.

What had she been playing at? The kiss had messed everything up.

She'd struggled to answer his text. They'd moved beyond words.

She felt the wedding ring on her right finger.

Yesterday, she'd been someone else for a little while. But when he saw her for what she really was, red-faced in her chef clothes barking orders at some kitchen porter; that would be the end of it.

And that was fine, she lied to herself.

The van arrived at Freshwater Bay just after lunch and Beth a little later, making record time in the old car.

Gareth, who'd been keeping an eye out for her from the flat above the restaurant, had re-assembled her bed so that all she needed to do was unpack her stuff.

She had all the basic things she needed on the van to fit out the apartment; table and chairs, a sofa, a chest of drawers, and boxes and boxes of kitchen equipment and store cupboard ingredients.

He was amazed. His kitchen stuff consisted of a wooden spoon, a fish slice and a bottle of sweet chilli sauce.

He'd bought her some groceries and put them in the fridge so she wouldn't need to think about shopping. He also popped a bottle of champagne in there as a welcome present.

As a last-minute thought, on the table he'd filled a catering size silver tin can he found with a bunch of wildflowers and forget-me-nots that were growing in the hedgerow.

What was he doing? He threw them in the bin.

Press reset, he reminded himself. He would leave as soon as he could after she arrived. He wouldn't apologise or even mention the kiss. He'd try and act normally and let things cool off between them.

His body though hadn't read the playbook. And he felt his pulse start to race when he saw the little silver hatchback pulling into the restaurant car park.

He rushed down to greet her as she got out of the car.

She smiled a little shyly as she walked over to him by the restaurant door.

He was torn.

What should he do? Hug her? Peck her on each cheek? No, best not to kiss her. Or wrap her in his arms.

He saw her head cocking slightly as she approached.

"Hey!"

He had to play it cool.

"Hi."

She went to kiss him, but last minute he lifted his head and she gave him a brief hug.

She looked a little disappointed as she stepped away.

"Good trip?"

"Yeah."

He handed her the set of keys

"I believe that these belong to you now."

She studied him for a moment, like she was assessing the situation between them.

Then turning away from him, she gave an excited whoop as she went inside.

"So... this is what it's like to own a restaurant!"

She spread her arms out in the middle of the dining area and twirled.

Gareth couldn't help but laugh.

Beth's phone rang out.

"It's Harry Hops, " she said, answering it, "I'm meeting him later."

Gareth leaned back against a table and waited for Beth to finish the call.

"Oh my God... No! Stop it, you're joking... no! .... *Harry!*"

Gareth watched her giggling into the phone. She certainly

seemed to be settling in well with the people around here.

Harry was quite full of himself; a bit of a bragger. He was a popular lad in the local rugby team. They'd played together a fair bit. They'd even gone kayaking together once, but Harry preferred doing more extreme stuff like cliff diving and free climbing.

And he was always chasing the girls.

He'd seen how Beth's face had lit up when she saw his name on the call. He was sure she was flirting with him.

"OK, see you in a bit... You too... Bye."

Who was Beth Barnes, sorry, Beth Morgan? Truth was, he realised, he didn't much know.

She had gone through with the marriage. But only so she could have the restaurant. She'd agreed to this deal so she could, like him, still be single and a free agent.

Maybe she was making that point to him now?

A kiss meant nothing. It was lucky he'd decided to press pause on this thing between them.

She was walking over to him. It was time for him to go.

"Sorry about that, Gareth. Harry's coming over later to discuss the brewery contract."

"No worries," he said, glancing at his watch.

"I'll let you get settled in. I've a couple of fixes to do in the boathouse. I'll see you around."

Inside, Beth was alone. Gareth had gone. He'd avoided a kiss and hugged like an old friend.

She'd have been humiliated if it was anyone else, but perhaps he was embarrassed too about yesterday. They'd gotten carried away.

Bloody tango.

But then, after she'd ended the call, he had that proud, hard mouth about him again. Like when they'd first met. Closed-off. Cold.

She was surprised, but he was probably regretting their kiss. She hoped that it wouldn't make things strange between them.

Oh, well. It obviously had.

She stood in the restaurant and wasted no time in systematically noting the things she wanted to change and what jobs she needed to do. Ariana would be able to advise, she was sure.

There were some great original features. The seating booths were expensive, real leather. The lighting was original French too. Globe sidelights set in brass fittings on the walls, with matching chandeliers in the central section. Beth was glad about that. Lighting could cost serious money.

She'd got some savings from working, and after her mum had died but she'd need to finance the first few weeks. She had no choice but to keep a tight rein on refurbishment costs.

The restaurant was nice enough, but it did lack the drama of the restaurants she'd worked in.

She stared at the floor space. What if she created an opening between the restaurant and the kitchen, a front pass for the head chef to work at and the food to go out from?

It would create a focal point. The customers could see into the busy kitchen from a distance and it wouldn't use any precious restaurant floor space. Then, if she subdivided the kitchen behind, she could create a more private space for washing up and prep.

She wondered how expensive that would be? She wished Gareth was here, she could do with his advice.

As she was making a list of the jobs, there was a knock at the restaurant window. A tall, blond man was peering in.

Beth noticed his swagger as he strode inside.

"Hey, Beth. Great to meet you."

Harry Hops took off his Oakley sunglasses and looked her up and down. She held out her hand and he gave it a firm shake holding onto it to lean in for a double kiss on both cheeks.

Beth stepped away from him.

"Awesome place you got here."

They sat at a booth as Harry launched into a long tale about his business and how he made and blended his craft beers. Beth listened, not able to get a word in. But it was interesting. Brewing was certainly a skilled and complex process, and she liked the sound of his unusual flavourings.

The Kiwi knew his stuff alright. And he hadn't once paused for breath.

He quoted her some competitive prices and suggested some ideas for the bar pumps which he told her he'd fit for free.

It all sounded good.

"So are we in business, or what?" he asked when he finally wound up talking.

She was feeling a little steamrollered. Harry wasn't going from there without a deal.

"I like what you do, but I wanna taste them first."

"Good as gold. How 'bout you come over to the micro-brewery tomorrow arvo. I'll give you a tour. You can try them out, then."

Beth agreed. Harry was a talker, alright. And he carried on talking to her all the way out of the restaurant to his van.

After leaving Beth, Gareth went back to the boathouse. The fixes he had to do were an excuse. He sat on the deck, 'thinking' for a while.

His mother called it brooding.

He was trying his best to shake himself free of the dejection he was feeling but it lay around him like a sea fog.

What had happened?

It was only a phone call. But it was her tone. She was flirting. Like she had with him.

She obviously had others hooks in the water.

And she'd reeled him in too.

Well, if Beth was up for it, there was no point sitting here and watching on, while Harry made his moves. He'd go up there now and see her.

She was like an itch he needed to scratch. He'd ask her straight out if she was up for a change of terms? A 'friends with benefits' kind of thing? If it was anything like that tango, they'd be mind-blowing together.

What did he have to lose? She'd taken a chance on him before.

She might even be grateful. It could work for both of them. It would help him get her out of his system.

He locked up the boathouse and began to make his way back up the lane to the restaurant.

The high hedgerows hid him from sight as he climbed up the sandy track. And he was nearly at the car park when he first caught sight of Beth.

She was coming out of the restaurant with Harry. He was talking to her as they both went towards his van. She was nodding.

Things certainly appeared to be very friendly between them.

Gareth ducked lower out of sight as Harry's words drifted over the hedge.

"Great to meet ya, Beth. So tomorrow arvo, then? I'll swing by at four?"

What was that? A date?

And then an embrace. Kisses on the cheeks. Was that in keeping with a business meeting?

Harry was hitting on her.

And she was lapping it up.

He was right. She *was* a player.

And *man*, had he been played.

Just like Chantelle.

He'd seen enough.

Dodging out of sight of the car park, he jogged back down to the boathouse and slammed the door shut behind him.

The overly long embrace Harry had given her before he got into his van overpowered her.

In spite of that, Beth felt encouraged by the meeting. It was a good start.

She spent the rest of the afternoon checking out the kitchen equipment. Much to her relief, it was all working perfectly.

Then she counted the cutlery and plates. She needed to change those.

It was nearly nine, and the sun was setting when she went upstairs into the apartment itself.

It was bigger than she could ever have imagined. There was a spacious lounge with wall to wall windows. Like the restaurant, there were wonderful views of the bay and the islands beyond.

It also looked down directly onto the boathouse.

That was irritating.

It meant she could see if Gareth was there, which would only make her wonder what he was up to.

She snapped the curtains shut tight. She wasn't about to become his stalker any time soon.

Walking around the boxes, she noticed that Gareth had been busy. He'd put her bed together for her in the largest bedroom. That was nice of him.

She found her pillows and quilt and made up the bed. There were four good sized bedrooms in all. There was more than enough space for when her friends came to stay. Although she didn't own a spare bed yet, she hoped that Alys and Jo would come and see her.

The bathroom was old fashioned with a big cast iron bath that would take ages to fill. But there was a serviceable shower in it. The kitchen was well equipped with worn antique pine units. It would do her fine until she could afford to renovate.

The flat was much bigger than anywhere she'd lived before, including her mum's old terraced house. It was weird thinking that this was where Evan had lived with Monique for all those years. The place had a warmth about it that she couldn't explain. It made her feel peaceful.

Evan had given her an amazing gift.

She opened the fridge.

Gareth had bought her food. He'd even got her a bottle of champagne. She should call him and say thank you.

Peeking through the curtains, she noticed the lights in the boathouse suddenly go dark.

It would keep until tomorrow.

As would unpacking the boxes.

CHAPTER 17

----------*---------

B eth was stacking and covering the restaurant furniture
when Ariana arrived at the restaurant the next morning.
"In here."

Ariana rushed over and embraced Beth.

"I'm *so* glad you're back. I was super-excited after you told me.
You'll love it here."

Beth showed her around and explained her plans to see what
Ariana thought.

Afterwards, Ariana spent time roaming around, sizing the
space. She agreed, it needed more light. And opening up the kitchen frontage was a no-brainer.

"Yeah, vintage tiles sound cool. A muted dove grey and a light
sage would work great with that. You *so* need big mirrors. Make
it *real* Frenchy. We can do it on the cheap by mocking up some
gilded frames. I'd be happy to do those for you... And Oh My
Gosh! You have to put a navy teal around the bar. It'll so bring
out that wood. And the bar itself, it's gotta be a feature. Wooden
mouldings. Make it look antique."

She certainly had an eye for detail.

It was the same eye for detail that noticed Beth's finger as she
absently removed her rubber gloves to jot her ideas down.

"*Holy shit!*"

Beth's biro paused mid-word.

Ariana was staring at her hand.

She glanced down and then realised.

"Coffee?"

Beth took Ariana up to the kitchen in the apartment, where she'd unpacked the kettle and a couple of mugs. She made them both a strong coffee.

There was nowhere to go with this. She figured it was best to come clean.

"If I tell you, you really mustn't say anything. For the sake of Ellen and David."

She hoped she could trust her. There was no option but to.

"Gareth doesn't want anyone to find out, especially his parents. Please. Swear it, Ariana."

"I won't tell a soul. I promise. Your secret's safe with me."

Ariana listened intently while Beth told her about the conditions Evan had placed on the inheritance. She explained their plan of a marriage of convenience, re-stressing the need to keep it a secret to spare the family any embarrassment if and when they found other partners and decided to end things.

"Please don't judge us, Ariana. This is purely business. It's an opportunity."

Ariana considered what she'd told her.

"Gareth came into the studio two weeks ago acting a bit odd. He wanted a ring for his mother's birthday, he said. Straight away, he picked out your ring. But I wouldn't sell it to him."

"Why not?"

"I've got this strange thing about some of the jewellery. You're going to think I'm a loon now, so don't laugh, right. I've got this thing with some pieces. Like a sixth sense. Especially the Celtic ones. Can't explain it."

Ariana scowled.

"Don't mock. Some of those rings, *they* seem to choose their owners."

Beth burst into giggles.

"*What!* Like Harry Potter's wand?"

Ariana threw her a look.

"You think I'm crazy... then *this* happens."

She shrugged at Beth.

"Go figure."

Ariana drew a breath.

"Anyhows, I told Gareth he couldn't have it 'cos I knew Ellen was a size seven finger. David bought her an eternity ring last year. You and that ring are both a six. But he wouldn't give up. He wanted it anyway and gave me some old blarney about it going on Ellen's pinkie."

Her eyes widened.

"What woman wears a ring like that on their pinkie, right? He's a pathetic liar. But, argh, a sale's a sale. And he was pushy. So I sold it to him, and then I felt bad about it after. And now, you're here, back in Freshwater Bay. Wearing *that* ring."

Ariana paused and studied Beth closely.

"Not on the proper finger, honey... but something tells me you guys are working on that."

Beth blushed.

What did Ariana know?

Anyhow, she'd not heard from Gareth since he'd given her the keys. She'd scared him off.

It was over between them, and that was probably for the best. He'd gotten his land and she'd gotten the restaurant.

They'd kissed. So what? Chapter closed.

"Really, Ariana. This is *just* a business deal."

Gareth had spent the whole evening sulking.

Leaving the boathouse early the next morning to work on a roofing job, he looked up at the restaurant apartment and could see that the curtains were open.

She must have gotten up early. Or, perhaps, she wasn't there?

Could it be that the cocky Kiwi phoned her back and had taken her out to dinner? Perhaps they'd gone back and drank the champagne he'd bought her?

What if, right now, she was in Harry's bed, doing all the things he'd imagined they'd do together?

There was half a day's work to do on the roof, but by mid-afternoon, he'd banged his finger three times and broken far too many slates from hitting them too hard.

He needed to get his head straight and put things into perspective. He told himself to think about Madog and the crappy hand he'd been dealt. Madog had to cope every day with losing Caitlin every day.

He'd see if his mother would babysit Jake so they could go out for a drink.

There was no point contacting Beth. She had her Saturday night sorted with Harry Hops.

She hadn't texted or called but he'd gotten the message.

Loud and clear.

Ellen was feeding the lambs when Gareth came over. He gave her a wave as he came into the shed.

He'd been so much happier recently, but he had that surly look about him again today; the one he got when something was getting to him.

He was so deep, that boy.

But for all the thinking he did, he could never get his head around his feelings very well. He was always squashing things down. Toughing it out. Keeping his problems to himself.

What was it this time?

She wondered if he'd met Anwen, the schoolteacher yet? Anwen had told Ellen when they chatted in the shop that she went into the Lobster Pot from time to time with her friends.

Ellen had hinted to her about Gareth. She'd even sent her a message, asking when she was free to come round for supper one night. Anwen still hadn't got back to her with a date, like she'd promised.

She'd send her a reminder, she decided. She'd invite her tomorrow for a roast beef dinner. And invite Gareth too.

Put her under his nose.

"Mam, can you look after Jake tonight, so me and Madog can go to the Lobster Pot?"

Ellen nodded.

"No problem. Come for dinner tomorrow night, love. I'm cooking a roast."

Gareth agreed but he still looked sullen.

She'd found that when things bothered the boys, it was always best to give them a job.

"D'you mind taking the tractor out for an hour for us, son? Dad's got Jake and we need some weeds topping in the bottom fields."

"Sure."

Ellen watched him go out of the shed towards the tractor.

Chantelle had been bad news, but a little help from her was all that boy needed and he'd be right as rain again. And this time, with a nice Welsh girl.

Gareth was glad to have something else to concentrate on. He got the tractor out and meticulously drove up and down the fields for two hours cutting the grass; concentrating on the line of the tractor and making sure he'd cut down every thistle and nettle.

Strangely, by the time he'd parked the tractor back in the shed, his mood had lifted and he was feeling more optimistic.

Madog was coming in from the fields too. He drove over to Gareth on his farm quad bike with two border collie dogs in tow.

Gareth bent down to pat one of the collies.

"Everything alright with the sheep?"

Madog switched off the engine.

"Yeah fine. Got some holes in the fence where badgers have been. Need to fix that tomorrow or the lambs'll be getting out."

This was Madog's world.

He knew every inch of the land, every animal, every fence. He was fortunate as the youngest son to be farming. Traditionally, it would have been Gareth, the eldest who'd have taken over the farm.

But from a young age, Gareth was always the architect. From Lego and Meccano toys to technical drawings and computer designed builds.

Still, he was happy to help out when needed. He quite enjoyed being out in the fields or milking the cows.

Madog grinned at him.

"Did Mam put you on the tractor?"

Gareth nodded, handing him the keys.

Madog looked him in the eye.

"Everything alright?"

Gareth focussed on the collie sitting patiently at his side.

"Yeah. Why?"

"Ah, nothing. You can tell me about whatever it is later... How was London?"

Gareth started making a fuss of the dog.

"Ah, London's London. Busy. Full of people rushing around."

"And did they like your designs?"

Gareth cleared his throat. He hated lying.

"Uhh... yeah. It went well. Sorry, I'm gonna have to go. Gotta get a shower. Mam's babysitting. What time d'you wanna meet up?"

CHAPTER 18

----------*---------

The Lobster Pot Inn was bursting at the seams. The place had gotten a whole heap quieter since the new landlord had taken over a couple of years ago, but it still had live bands playing some weekends. And tonight it looked like everyone had turned out to party.

Beth had arranged to meet Ariana there after the brewery tour and she was looking forward to ditching Harry as soon as she got back to Freshwater Bay.

He kept making suggestive comments as they wandered around the plant. She'd ignored those, but she was annoyed that she'd had to spend the whole time fending him off. He'd kept on trying to touch her and when he'd tried to put his arm around her she'd given him a hard stare. She tried to be polite. His beers were great and Harry had real talent. It was a shame he was such a creep.

As he drove them into the Lobster Pot car park, Beth made her excuses to leave. She wanted to do a deal with Harry but she'd had enough of him hitting on her. She'd speak to him about that again. In a daytime meeting with a big table between them.

Harry parked up. She made her move to get out and go but Harry got out too.

"Thanks for the tour, Harry. Your beers are really original."

She was ditching him anyway, she decided.

She closed the van door and turned to walk away towards the

pub.

"I'll give you a call so we can discuss terms."

He grabbed her arm.

"Hey! Wait up, Beth..."

She pulled away and shook it free, glaring at him not to dare do that again.

Bang.

His face smashed into the side of the van.

From nowhere, Gareth had charged in, overpowering Harry.

He was now pinned by Gareth's shoulder with his cheek squashed hard against the side door, his arm locked behind his back.

Harry was shouting out in pain as Gareth was pressing in harder, twisting his arm further up his back.

Beth watched on in horror.

"Gareth! What you playin' at? Let go of him. Now!"

Gareth turned his head to look at her.

She was shaking with fury. How dare he!

Seeing how mad she was, Gareth dropped his vice-like hold. Shoving Harry into the van door he turned to march from there.

Quick as a flash, Harry whipped around. He sprang forward to grab Gareth from behind but Beth saw him coming and stepped in between them.

She stared Harry down and he stopped in his tracks.

When she was in this mood they better not mess with her. And she wasn't about to mince her words.

What gave Gareth the right to go attacking Harry like that? She'd been in control of the situation, and she'd handled far worse than him.

She glared at Harry and he shrunk back, rubbing his wrists.

"Stay there. Don't even think about it."

She strode over to Gareth who'd skulked away to the harbour wall.

"Who the Hell d'you think you are? My keeper?"

Gareth said nothing.

"You're like a *bloody caveman*. You know the terms. You wrote them. You don't own me, Gareth Morgan. We're free agents, re-member."

His hard jaw was clamped tight, his angry eyes drilled deep into hers.

She shook her head, turned on her heels and marched back to Harry.

Gareth watched her from the harbour wall as she made a point, rather dramatically and for his benefit no doubt, of checking that Harry was alright.

The Kiwi bastard was lapping it up as she all but mopped his brow. He even threw Gareth a cheeky wink as she led him away from the van and into the pub.

Bollocks!

Sitting down on the bench, Gareth put his head in his hands.

How could things go this wrong this quickly?

He'd been walking down to the Lobster Pot when he saw them getting out of the van.

Harry had grabbed her arm.

He hadn't thought. He'd just piled in.

She'd warned him off like he was some jealous ex. Worse than that. Like he was her stalker.

Was he going to go into the pub or not?

Madog was waiting for him in the back bar.

Why should he change his plans? He had every right to be there. And he wasn't about to go hiding from her. Like she said, they were free agents. And this was his place, not hers.

He rubbed and stretched his knuckles.

He'd keep out of her way. And if she was still hanging around, well he'd have a bit of fun too. Make *her* a little jealous for a change. See how she felt about that?

The lounge bar had quietened down by the time Beth wandered into the Lobster Pot with Harry. The band was starting to play in the back bar and the crowd had moved through.

She found a table and Harry got them a drink.

"What's that prick, Gareth, to you, anyways?"

"Business partner."

Harry sneered.

"Looks like he wants to be more than that."

Beth didn't comment.

"Harry, there's only one reason I came in here with you."

He gave her a sleazy look.

"Babe, if I'd've known, I'd've taken you back to mine. Saved us all that hassle."

Beth ignored that. But, she was done with being nice.

"I really like your products. What I don't like is you. If you carry on harassing me with your sexist come-ons, there's no deal. D'you get it? Harry, I mean it. You treat me with respect or we're done. D'you understand?"

Harry looked at her confused.

Suddenly his face broke into an enlightened grin.

"No worries. I get it."

"Good. Call me Monday morning and we'll sort the terms."

With the conversation drying up quickly after that, it wasn't long before Harry abandoned her on a pretext.

Relieved, she watched him go through to the back bar.

It didn't matter where she was, London or even out here in Freshwater Bay, she was such a goon magnet. What was wrong with her?

Spotting Beth sitting alone, Ariana gave her a shout to come over to the side of the lounge bar.

"It's mad next door and Marcus has got me working. Ever been behind a bar?"

"'Course."

"Hop on then will ya, and give us a hand for a sec."

Marcus, the landlord gave her a grateful nod as she started serving drinks.

From behind the bar, she could see Gareth over in a quieter corner by the pool table. Next to him was a young man with similar features. He was dark and had the same chiselled jaw, but he was slighter and more wiry in build. Madog, she guessed.

Thankfully, they hadn't noticed her and she was enjoying being busy. It wasn't quite so crazy once she'd started serving too, and as she poured the pints of beer she could people watch. Between serving customers, she kept a beady eye on Gareth.

Madog kept coming up for lager and tequila shots at the other end of the bar. Ariana had served him each time. They were going for it with the drinks.

At one point, she saw Harry squaring up to Gareth aggressively. Gareth stood his ground. Pool cue in hand. He'd been about to take a shot.

For a second, she worried that it might kick off between them again, but it was quickly over. Harry said something to him, then went back to a group of rugby lads at the other end of the bar.

A while later, she was back to watching Gareth again. He'd been drinking and playing pool all evening, but over the last few minutes there'd been a new development. And it began to bug Beth; big time.

A young woman was hanging around the pool table, and she was clearly flirting with him. There was nothing subtle about her. Fake-tan orange; she wore tight Daisy Duke shorts with high platform sandals. Her tight vest top showed off an impressive pair of beach-ball shaped surgically-enhanced boobs which she pushed out as she threw her head back.

Beth sneered as she poured a beer. It was pathetic. The girl was laughing like a loon at everything Gareth said to her.

Beth took the money for the round of drinks she'd served then cast her eyes back towards the pool tables again. Tan Tits was sucking on the straw of her bottled cider, flicking her platinum blonde long hair back and sidling up even closer to Gareth.

Feeling a little nauseous, Beth looked away. She was tormenting herself by watching them.

Unable to resist, a few minutes later she checked him again.

Fake-Bake Barbie was still there. She was playing pool now with Madog.

Beth watched on as she bent over the table in her hot-pants.

Shit! Gareth was looking straight at her.

He'd seen her spying on him.

With his eyes steadily on Beth, he leaned right over Barbie, far too closely for Beth's liking, showing her the angle of the shot.

His mouth was inches from her neck. His body next to hers. His taunting face stared at Beth like a drunken vampire about to take a bite.

Bastard! He was rubbing it in her face.

She'd seen enough.

Now the bar had slackened off, she found Ariana.

"The move and everything, it's catching up with me. I'm whacked. I'm off home, sorry."

Ariana hugged her.

"Want me to walk you back?"

"No. Don't be daft. This is Freshwater Bay, not London. I'll be fine."

She needed to clear her head.

Dashing out of the pub's side door, she wandered through the streets behind the harbour for a while as she tried to reason with herself. Why was she boiling with rage?

She'd seen Gareth getting with a girl. That was the agreement. They were free agents, as she'd reminded him in the car park.

So, why then, did it hurt so much?

Gareth had been in the back bar with Madog. They'd been lining up the drinks as soon as they got in.

He was still angry after his brush with Harry Hops and he sank his first pint in seconds, then ordered another. He wanted to get drunk and forget the clusterfuck that was Beth Barnes.

The band was loud, the bar was crowded and he'd slammed way too much tequila.

To distract himself from thinking about Beth with that brash Kiwi, he was at the pool tables where there was more space and they could play a few games.

He'd been about to take a shot when Harry stormed over. He was on a mission, like he was about to throw a punch.

Gareth flexed and stood his ground.

"What the fuck do you want now?"

Harry laughed scornfully in his face.

"Came to tell ya yer wastin' yer time with that chef, yer prick."

"What?"

"Beth Barnes, mate. She's a fuckin' lesbian."

Having said what he came to say, Harry retreated back to his rugby mates.

Beth wasn't gay, he was sure. And she wasn't with Harry anymore. That was about all that registered in Gareth's tequila-fogged brain.

And then he saw her there, and he couldn't take his eyes off her. What was she doing pulling pints?

He slammed down yet another shot and took a long swig of the lager Madog had brought back from the bar.

No texts. No calls from her. Tonight, she'd made it clear exactly where they stood. That kiss counted for nothing. He was nothing to her.

He sneered. Maybe he wasn't her keeper, but he was still her bloody husband.

That was a joke.

Annie Airbags came over. She'd been in high school with Madog and she joined them playing pool.

Named after her impressive boob job, Annie Airbags was a tease. But she was like that with everyone. He liked her well enough, but not in *that* way. It didn't matter how drunk he got, he'd never go there.

Beth was watching them as she served. Even from across the room he could see she was scowling at him. So, he hammed it up a bit to see what she'd do next.

Bending a little too closely over Annie, he breathed onto her neck and moved the cue for her as he helped her pick out the shot. Not that he was much use at pool by now.

Two of us can tango, sweetheart.

He slammed another tequila or two with Madog and Annie, then got a little distracted in conversation.

He turned his attention back to the bar. Where was she?

Shit! She'd gone.

The harbourfront was empty. Only a couple of smokers stood chatting by the front door.

The fresh air hit him and his stomach flipped. He was one second away from heaving his guts.

He sat down on the bench in the harbour and bent over double, trying to control the waves of nausea washing over him.

He was pissed.

He raised his head and blinked. The air was still, but the boats in front of him were spinning. Even the restaurant on the clifftop was moving. That wasn't normal. He was an architect, he knew about shit like that.

She was probably back there now.

"S'a good sign," he told the harbour wall, mumbling to himself on the bench. "She's pissed off. That means she likes me."

He should strike while the iron's hot. Go up there now and ask her if she fancied a shag.

How would that go down?

The ground reared up in front of him as he got to his feet and he grabbed the harbour wall to steady himself.

His stomach lurched and he spewed its contents over the side into the sea.

Staggering precariously onto the jetty he stepped unsteadily onto his boat.

A little sleep first.

Then he'd go.

CHAPTER 19

----------✳--------

It was nine in the morning and the sun had made the deck of the boat warm already.

Emerging from the cabin below Gareth squinted with pain as the bright light hit his face. His head was pounding. He hadn't felt this rough since his uni days.

He'd been going for it. A good idea at the time, but what had he been thinking? And he'd puked.

He rubbed his head in his hands. Remembering. Cringing.

Thank God he hadn't gone to see Beth. She'd have slapped him. Quite rightly too.

Idiot!

He should never have wound her up like that. She probably thought he'd gone with Annie.

Why did he do that?

He rubbed his stubbly chin.

He'd so screwed up.

This *'business arrangement'* business was harder than it looked. His head hurt.

He needed to get back to the boathouse, have a shower. Drink coffee. Curl up and die.

There wasn't a cloud in the sky and the sea was flat. If he didn't have the mother of all hangovers, it'd be the perfect day for an afternoon paddle and swim.

But, *boy*, was he rough.

He retreated back to the cabin for painkillers, water and more sleep.

Beth woke up still seething about the night before. And what really rubbed salt into the wounds was that when she opened the curtains, she could see the outside lights of the boathouse still on.

He hadn't been home.

He'd stayed over with Fake-bake Tits. Spent the night bouncing on those beach-balls.

She shook herself.

He'd been making the point to her. Their marriage was a sham.

Get over it, she told herself sternly. She had to get used to seeing him with other women. It was what they'd agreed.

And what did she care? She had this place.

After a cup of coffee, she started on her list. Today's job was deep cleaning the restaurant kitchen and she took on the challenge with vigour.

She scrubbed furiously through the morning. Cleaning was cathartic, she repeated to herself. And it was working. She did feel her anger draining away as she scoured and polished.

Still, Gareth had been a total arse. First, treating her like she was some sort of damsel in distress, and then making her jealous. That was cruel.

By early afternoon she'd brushed away her anger and the stainless steel in the kitchen was now gleaming. The fridges were all disinfected and Beth was finishing off degreasing the large extractor fans above the stoves.

it was not a job for the faint-hearted. This was obviously not Evan's favourite task. And whilst the kitchen wasn't in bad shape considering that it had been empty for a few years, the fans were filthy.

Black bits fell into her hair and grease dripped onto her face as she scraped above her to get the fat down.

But, eyes on the prize, she'd persevered and the fans were now spotless.

It was after one o'clock when Gareth rolled up to the restaurant with a double kayak in the back of his pickup. He was feeling human again. And after a slow start, he wasn't going to waste any more of a peachy day like this one.

He wasn't sure if she'd even speak to him after last night. But he had to give it a go.

He wanted to take her along the peninsula past the stack where there was a small beach only reachable by boat. He presumed she'd never been in a kayak, so it wasn't too difficult a paddle for her first go. And he needed no reminding that she could swim. He still thought about that a lot.

But it was better not to go out to the islands with her until she'd had some practice and done a couple of Eskimo rolls.

Hearing a metal scraping noise, he went through to the kitchen.

She'd been busy. The place sparkled.

"You had lunch yet?" he called out cheerfully.

Straight ahead of him was Beth.

Bottom in the air, she was kneeling on top of the stove. With one foot on the deep fat fryer, her head was inside the extractor hood. She was trying single-handedly to put the metal baffle plate back on.

"Dammit."

"Let me give you a hand with that."

Beth tried to turn but wobbled and Gareth rushed over to steady her.

He heard her huffing, her head still inside the fan as he stretched his arms up and took one side of the baffle.

Thank God he'd not gone to see her last night. He wasn't ever going to drink tequila again.

Together they put the metal panel back into place. It was a

two-man job and he was surprised that she had done the others on her own. That was Beth for you.

As she climbed back down, he took in the sight of her.

"Been enjoying yourself?"

She looked over at him, real mean, filling him with a sickening dread that she was probably going to tell him where to go.

Covered pretty much head to her shoulders in old cooking grease and black bits, she was going to need a long hot shower.

But right now, she needed something to wipe that grease up. He was sure he had some paper towels in the cab of his truck.

Turning around, he quickly left to go get them.

"Fantastic! Yeah, go on. Walk away," she shouted as she heard the door shutting behind him.

He was gone like a shot when he'd seen the state of her. And who'd blame him? The tango temptress was now grease girl, she lamented shaking her hair violently into the large dustbin, trying to get the worst of the bits out.

"Hero to bloody zero in three days flat. A record, even for me," she muttered loudly.

The bubble had well and truly popped. He'd seen her, finally for what she was. As she really was. And like all the other men in her life, predictably he'd vanished too.

Sniffing, she bent and shook her hair over the bin.

"Well, that's fine with me, Buster," she grumbled, sharing her anger with the black plastic. "You go tango with that inflated orange Barbie doll you were probably bonking all night. Just don't expect to come to *my* restaurant afterwards and ask *me* to cook you and Big Tits dinner."

She stood back up.

Gareth was standing there. A wad of paper towels in his hands.

"I thought you might be needing these."

He held one out for her to take.

"Save spoiling your towels."

Oh God! Beth cringed.

Not only did she look like she'd dipped her head in the deep fat fryer, he'd heard every word of her jealous rant.

Straightening up proudly, she took it from him and started wiping the grease off her cheek.

"Tell me you didn't hear all that?"

His face was impenetrable.

"What? The bonking part or the bit about cooking for me and Big Tits?"

She sniffed, embarrassed as his face cracked into a broad smirk.

"Yeah, well, you weren't meant to hear that... I was talking to the bin."

"Beth, about last night. When I saw you'd gone, I went after you. But you'd disappeared and I was drunk. I slept it off on the boat. Alone."

She stared at him blankly, refusing to break.

Moving closer towards her, with a paper towel he reached across and gingerly brushed an ancient fragment of black chip off the tip of her nose.

His eyes met hers.

"I'm sorry, Beth. I'm never like that. I treated you really badly last night. I don't know what came over me. I was jealous."

Her lips pinched as she considered carefully what he'd said.

"Jealous?"

His eyes fixed on hers and her traitorous heart thumped hard.

"I told Harry where to go."

"He thinks you're gay."

She couldn't help but catch Gareth's grin and he handed her another paper towel.

"You're not, are you?"

She shook her head, then cleaned her face clear of the last of the dirt.

He took the towels off her and put them in the bin.

"So, how you feeling today?" she asked.

"Better now."

She looked at him sternly.

"Was the wrong answer?" he said, taking his cue from her. "Oh! I get it... Yeah. I'm feeling terrible. Real rough."

"What?" she pursued. "Like with a really, really bad headache?"

"Like the worst ever. I've slept all morning. Haven't been able to keep food down. Been dosing myself up with painkillers. Sworn never to touch another drop of tequila as long as I live."

"Good. I'm very glad to hear that you've been suffering."

She screwed her nose.

"Wanna start over?"

"Please. Let's draw a line under one crappy evening."

She nodded and his face broke into a broad toe-curling smile that made her suddenly self-conscious.

"Look at me. I'm a right sight."

She took a deep sniff of her t-shirt.

"And I smell even worse."

"Actually, you look kinda cute."

She backed away from him, her chin high. She was still wary, he could tell.

"I hope that wasn't you flirting with me, pal."

"After the way you sorted Harry Hops out last night? I wouldn't dare."

He sniffed.

"I'm not gonna lie though, you do smell like a chip shop."

He laughed and dodged out of the way as she tried to rub his face in one of the soiled paper towels from the bin.

"OK, greasy. Hit the shower. Then we're off for a paddle, if you're up for it?"

"Cool."

"Put on a T-shirt, shorts, flip flops. Things you don't mind getting wet."

He grinned at her.

"Swimsuit's optional."

It was a glorious day to be on the water. They'd had a wobbly start in the kayak because Beth kept mucking about and giggling.

"You're gonna tip us if you keep trying to splash me," he warned.

Because he was by far the heaviest and more experienced, he sat in the rear seat and this gave her the ideal opportunity to pretend to paddle and keep splashing him in the face.

"Very funny."

"Just getting my own back for last night," she said, facing forward.

"Did I tell you I puked up?"

"Glad I didn't hang around to see that."

Once they got their rhythm, they got out onto the open sea and were soon paddling past the bay and along the cliffs of the peninsula.

Beth was in raptures. The views along the cliffs were spectacular. Sheets of sheer rocks towered above her in patinas of orange and grey, with layered strata jutting vertically into the turquoise blue.

Caves were peppered all along the cliffs like bullet holes whirled out by the waves.

They headed out towards a stack, a large piece of cliff that had become detached from the sea; a huge mass of sheer grey rock rising out of the water.

Beth spotted a little bird flying above her onto the side of the stack. A row of tiny fish packed tidily in its bright orange beak.

"A puffin," Gareth observed.

She stopped paddling to watch it fly to its nest on the side of the cliff face.

"Look, they're in flying school."

They floated on the water's surface, taking in the breathtaking view of the stack with hundreds of young puffins clinging to the cliff edge, taking turns to practise sorties over the sea.

The stack, rock arches, the caves and the seabirds; these were views only visible from the water and Beth felt blessed.

Gareth spoke behind her.

"I had a lucky escape as a baby. Dad says Mam tried to name me Puffin, but he put a stop to it. Thank God. Did you notice in the kitchen, it's full of puffin mugs and tea towels? The woman's obsessed."

Laughing at the idea of Ellen as 'the mad puffin woman' they paddled closer to the stack.

"Come on Puffy, get a wiggle on."

Gareth splashed her with the paddle.

"What is it with you? You keep making me tell ya stuff I know I'm gonna regret. Anyway, I'd've called myself Finn. That's a seriously cool name for a little adventuresome kayaker."

Beth agreed.

Gareth steered them carefully around the stack and they then paddled across to a small sandy bay hollowed out of the cliff and only accessible by boat.

They pulled the kayak onto the white sand. Gareth got out a waterproof bag and set out a rug, towels, a couple of sandwiches and two cans of lemonade.

They lay back on the rug and ate their picnic.

He was relieved they were friends again. And he was enjoying taking her out on the water, showing her all the places that he loved.

From what he could see, she enjoyed being outdoors, seeing the wildlife too. Freshwater Bay couldn't match London for entertainment but it certainly did have its own sights to see, if you knew where to look for them.

"Gareth, thank you for taking me here. It's so spectacularly beautiful and peaceful. I love it."

Gareth turned on his side towards her, looking down at her lying flat on the rug beside him. Dressed to tango, out for a paddle, even covered in grease, she was so damn sexy. And she was always surprising him.

"Glad you like it," he said, his voice catching.

His pulse raced as tilted her head towards him and their eyes met.

That spark again. Did she realise how much he wanted to kiss her?

Suddenly she shifted and sat up, breaking the spell.

"*Uhh*...This sun's so hot. I'm gonna burn. Fancy a swim?"

Gareth grinned cheekily at her.

"Only if it's like the last time."

She shot him a quirky look then peeled off her T-shirt and shorts.

"Race you."

He caught a glimpse of her perfect round butt cheeks popping out from under her black string bikini bottoms as she ran into the sea.

Like a greyhound after a rabbit, Gareth peeled off his top and dived in too.

They lay flat for a while, floating on top of the water, cooling down from the hot sun. Then, Beth swam around and began teasing Gareth by splashing him. He tried to retaliate but she was too fast.

She'd disappeared under the water.

He lost sight of her; he hoped she was alright. There was no current or rip. But he had no idea how strong a swimmer she was and they were treading water so she couldn't touch the seabed.

Suddenly; a sharp, fast tug on his shorts. They were around his shins, then his toes.

"Beth!"

Too late. She was powering back to shore.

"What you playing at? Bring me those back."

She shouted over to him from the rug on the beach.

"Now I get my dare."

He swam around for a couple of minutes contemplating his next move.

"You said swim naked in the sea. I'm doing it. We're quits. Now gimme my shorts back. Please."

"Alright. Come and get 'em."

What was she playing at?

"I'll close my eyes. Promise."

Taking the shorts down to the water's edge, she made a drama of going back to sit on the rug.

She screwed her eyes shut and covered them with her hands.

He shook his head. There was only one thing for him to do. And he had nowhere to hide.

Revenge was being served up cold alright, he thought grimly.

After waiting a minute or two, her face was still covered so he rushed out of the sea.

She was peeping. He could see her watching him sneakily, from under her fingers.

"Caught you."

The shorts still lay on the sand as he ran up the beach and grabbed her.

"You're peeking, you tinker."

Hoisting her over his shoulder in a fireman's lift, she squealed as he dumped her into the waves.

Then, with shorts back on, he joined her.

It was late afternoon by the time they'd paddled back.

Beth wasn't sure what was going on between them. They were friends messing about, but it was definitely more than that. Play-fighting, splashing each other, stripping off his trunks. He'd let her see all of him.

Every now and then, she'd catch his eye as he watched her. The fiery intensity she felt in them took her breath away. Whatever this was, it was thrilling.

Pulling alongside the slipway they got out and hauled the boat up the deck.

"Come on. I'll show you the boathouse."

She was more than a little curious to see what he'd done.

And she wasn't disappointed when she stepped inside. In fact, she was gobsmacked by the stylish Scandinavian-style living area he'd created.

"The high ceiling... and the windows with the sea all around. This is seriously cool."

Gareth grinned as she made her way over to the kitchen peninsula that divided the space behind the living area. She brushed her hand over the granite worktops.

"*Ahh*, this kitchen... it's spectacular."

Her eyes were drawn to the large, slate-coloured, state of the art range oven.

"A Kestrel Deluxe," she uttered as if in a trance.

He smirked.

"You are such a kitchen geek."

"So true. Nought to 200 degrees Celsius in three minutes flat. Self-cleaning ovens and an induction hob."

"You sound like my brother Owen with his new car."

As she bent down to open the doors he snuck up behind her. Nipping her waist he tickled her mercilessly as she fought back, bringing him down onto the floor with her.

She gazed up at him as they both suddenly calmed.

He was on his knees on top of her, both of his hands over her wrists by her head, pinning her to the floor.

Her heart raced, thrilled by the energy pulsing between them. His hooded eyes were focussed on her lips.

It's what they both wanted.

So why wouldn't he hurry up and kiss her?

She was on the floor under him. Her hair had come loose from the ponytail and fanned out around her head. Her cheeks were flushed.

He studied her lips. They were the most delicate rose pink. He wanted more than anything to taste them again.

The electricity crackled between them. They'd be so good together.

He checked himself.

He'd got it so wrong last night, before he kissed her again he had to be certain she wanted this too.

He moved his hand and released her.

His hand gently caressed her face, brushing away a strand of her hair.

He heard her breathing heavily as he shifted and lifted himself and her off the floor.

There was no way he was imagining it. The moment had passed, but now he was sure. She felt the same way as he did. But then, why hadn't she answered his texts. Or called him after she'd got here?

She straightened her t-shirt and fixed her hair.

They were both quiet. It felt a little awkward.

He turned his attention to picking the oven gloves off the floor.

Beth coughed.

"As I was saying, this cooker, my friend, is a thing of beauty."

Gareth rubbed his chin.

"What can I say? After you declared your undying love for range ovens, the budget option I'd picked looked a bit rubbish. It was a bitch to readjust the units but I'm glad I went for it. It's made a feature of the space."

"How does it cook?"

"Uh… I haven't switched it on yet."

She rolled her eyes at him and he felt the tension between them easing.

"To be fair, I've only been living here a week. I've used the induction hob a couple of times, but I've also been for dinner up at the farm."

The farm!

He'd been so wrapped up in Beth that he'd forgotten all about it. He was due up there right now for a Sunday roast beef dinner.

Beth smirked at him flirtily.

"How about we christen this baby, then?"

Gareth's eyes widened.

Did she even know what she was doing to him?

She'd ambled over to the fridge and was peering in, speaking to him with her head still inside it.

"It's the least I can do. You took me out on the water so I'll make you dinner."

Gareth raked his hand through his hair.

The farm was the last place he wanted to be, but he couldn't phone and cancel. Not this late. Not with his mother. He'd never hear the end of it.

"*Uhh*... sorry, Beth. I can't. I'd forgotten that Mam's invited me for dinner tonight."

She shut the fridge.

"Oh... okay... I'd better be getting back anyway. I've a chip fryer to sort out."

She was putting a brave face on but she sounded disappointed.

"Beth? Can we do it again, sometime soon?"

"Sure."

She slipped her flip flops on by the door.

"Thanks for the paddle, Gareth. I really enjoyed it."

She left soon after, and he watched her from the window as she walked quickly up the gravel track.

This was killing him.

CHAPTER 20

----------*----------

G areth changed and drove over to his parents' farm. Ellen had woken him from his sleep twice that morning reminding and insisting that he came over.

For the first time in his life, he could honestly say that he didn't give a toss about his mam's roast beef dinner. He wanted to stay with Beth and explore the contents of that black bikini.

Even worse, he spotted that this dinner was a bear trap as soon as he rolled up to the farm.

His heart sank. He was the bear.

A silver Mini Cooper was parked in the driveway. Ellen had guests. One to be precise. He could guess who it was. The schoolteacher.

Mam was interfering again.

He snuck quietly into the farmhouse by the side door they seldom used.

They usually ate in the kitchen. But tonight the table in the dining room had been set.

Mam was going for it. There were napkins laid beside the best cutlery. She'd got the crystal glasses out and there was a bottle of wine on the table.

He moved along the corridor and from the shadows of the hall he peered into the large living room they rarely used.

He heard his mother in there. And though he could only see her legs and sandals, there was a woman sitting with her. This

Anwen, he presumed. They were chatting together in Welsh.

He'd told her point-blank not to do this. At thirty-two years old, he did not need his mother to find him a girlfriend.

The last thing he wanted to do was to sit all evening with his mam embarrassing him in front of a woman he didn't care about. Especially when he could have been doing all sorts of things at this very moment with a woman he did.

Squashing his annoyance, he took some relief from the fact that he'd not been spotted.

He hung back and went in search of Madog.

The historic farmhouse was large with two wing extensions that had been added onto each side of the central living space.

Madog had taken one of the wings and had what could be loosely described as an apartment there.

He was settling Jake to sleep in his new cot when Gareth crept in.

Madog looked tired.

Seeing Gareth, he put his finger to his lips.

"How's your head this morning? Gareth whispered by the door.

"Bad. Dad did the milking. Where did you get to last night?"

"I need help."

"Mam's been cooking all afternoon."

"So, you know she's set me up?"

Madog yawned.

"What's she like?"

Gareth shook his head.

"Stunning... A very nice pair of sandals. That's all I could see. I can't stay. Can you take one for the team?"

"You'll be paying for this big-time tomorrow."

Gareth slapped his brother's back.

"I'll take my chances. Tell her whatever, just do us a favour and get her off my back for tonight."

Gareth Morgan was the most infuriating man she'd ever met,

Beth decided as she let herself into the restaurant and went upstairs to the flat.

It had all been going so well. Things had been building up between them all afternoon. Then, just as she thought he'd been about to kiss her again, he'd stopped.

Had to see his mother. Sunday roast dinner? What was that about?

What if he'd been lying and he had a date? He'd been with Fake-Bake, after all. And was going back for another bounce?

Drawing the curtains and those poisonous thoughts firmly shut, she caught sight of him leaving in his truck up the track.

Arghh! She was stalking him again.

She sighed and resigned herself to a night of unpacking her stuff.

So, it was a bit of a surprise when half an hour later her phone pinged with a text from the man himself.

> *'Hey, Beth. Change of plan. I'm outside in the pickup. You eaten yet? Fancy coming over and exploring the contents of my fridge again? BTW you're cooking ;)'*

She looked at herself in the full-length mirror propped up against her bedroom wall and tried to fix her hair. She was still in her kayaking clothes. She wasn't exactly ready to go out again.

She was in two minds about what to do about Mr Hot and Cold.

She'd had a great afternoon though. And the clincher; she badly wanted to try out that range cooker.

Without any more time to agonise over it, she went downstairs and locked the restaurant door behind her.

Gareth's face cracked into a dazzling smile as she opened the passenger door.

"Sorry to have messed you about. I'll tell you about it later."

She reached for her seat belt.

"I haven't had time to get changed."

"You always look stunning, Beth. Even covered in grease."

She took that as a joke and leaned back as he started the engine.

She had no idea what was going on in his head, but what harm could there be in cooking a little food and having a glass of wine?

He didn't have a lot in his fridge but Beth found some eggs, and a piece of chorizo and began making a Spanish style tortilla with a side salad.

Gareth sat by the worktops with his glass of Rioja watching her cook. She chopped up the onions and thinly sliced the potatoes like a machine.

When everything was cooked, she flipped the tortilla over effortlessly with a quick shuck of the pan. If he'd have done it, it would have been in pieces on the floor.

Soon she'd produced two plates of delicious food.

Beth sipped at her wine as Gareth ate another slice of her tortilla.

"I've been meaning to talk to you, Beth. About our arrangement."

She looked at him a little uncertainly.

"I've more or less finished the roof job now, so I'm free for a while if you need any work done on the restaurant. Seeing as we're partners and all? I'm happy to lend a hand."

"Seriously? That'd be awesome, " Beth answered gratefully. "Ariana's helping too."

"And you don't have to pay me. Just feed me."

"We'll see about that. I was thinking of knocking down part of a wall into the restaurant, so I could do with those muscles of yours."

Her eyes darted towards her wine glass and Gareth watched her cheeks turning crimson.

She cleared her throat.

"Gareth, I've got something I need to tell you too. About our arrangement."

She sounded serious. Had he been reading this wrong?

He jumped in.

"Beth, I want to apologise properly for last night. I dunno what came over me."

She shrugged.

"Hey, we both got the wrong end of the stick. You with Harry Hops. Me with Silicone Cindy. It's forgotten, already."

"You sure?"

"Yeah. Anyway, you more than made up for it today."

They both took another sip of wine.

"No, this is about Ariana," she continued. "She came over to see me and…"

She chewed at her lip.

"She recognised the ring, Gareth… She's sworn she won't tell anyone, but I'm worried she might. I'm sorry."

Gareth studied the ring on his right finger as he considered what she'd said.

"It'll be alright."

He reached over and touched her hand.

"Don't worry. I trust Ariana. She won't say a word."

They cleared the dirty dishes and moved out onto the deck. In the darkness above them, the stars were out.

Gareth brought out a thick rug and they lay on it, side by side, stargazing in peaceful silence.

"I've never seen so many stars, and as bright as this," she said wistfully, staring up.

"See those stars there? They're for you. Can you see them, in the shape of a saucepan, Chef."

He pointed them out with his arm.

She laughed silently.

"Yes. Trust you to find that for me."

"That's The Plough… If we're lucky we might see some shooting stars too."

"Wow, really?"

"You cold?"

He stretched his arm out above her head and she moved and snuggled up into him, her head resting on his shoulder. His arm wrapped around her. It felt so nice, listening to the waves, gazing up at the sky. The musky smell of his aftershave. The warmth of his body close to hers.

"I think I saw one," she uttered quietly, her pulse racing.

"Me too."

"My first shooting star."

Her heart pounded as she sensed his warm breath on her hair. Then, his mouth.

"You get to make a wish."

His lips brushed against her forehead.

"I do?" she breathed.

There was no way back now. They were in too deep.

She angled her head upwards close to his lips.

"Shall I tell you what I wished for?"

His mouth feverishly found hers.

The tip of their tongues touched, then tangled deeper as they kissed and made out passionately under the stars.

The heat between them was rising. Lust fired through her as he moved his lips greedily down her neck, his free hand hungrily exploring her body under her T-shirt. Her breasts, her stomach and down to her thighs. Her body thrummed with his touches in ravenous anticipation.

"Beth," he rasped, his breath jagged, "D'ya wanna? Ya know, change the terms?"

Suddenly coming to her senses, she broke away.

She had to be sure.

"But, you said you could never be with me?"

Gareth began kissing her neck again, coaxingly.

"Yeah, well, that was before. I was trying to protect you. Make sure you didn't have me pinned as your happily-ever-after guy."

He kissed her lips.

She pulled away.

"So, what are you, Gareth?"

He gave her a wolfish grin.

"How about, your right-here-right-now man?"

She giggled as he pulled her on top of him.

"I'm right here right now, to do anything you want me to."

He flipped her and covered her with more intoxicating kisses.

"Beth, seriously, from the first moment I saw you, I wanted you."

"You did?"

He nodded.

"Me too."

She gasped as he nipped her earlobe, shooting flares of passion through her. She didn't care about the arrangement, all she wanted was him. All of him.

"Let's go inside," he whispered into her ear. "Come to my bed."

"Not yet. I want you here, first. Under the stars."

"But Beth I don't..."

"Shh... I've got a coil."

He kissed her urgently, sending waves of shivers through her body, driving her wild with desire.

Moving his hands he stroked his way up, peeling off her T-shirt, releasing her bikini top so her breasts spilled out, and stripping her bare.

"So gorgeous."

His mouth covered them zealously, pebbling her nipples and driving her crazy.

"Shhh... relax."

Closing her eyes, she gave herself to him as his mouth moved southwards. He took her skilfully with his tongue until she cried out as he sent her skywards.

Then, it was her turn. Stripping him too, goosebumps broke out over his skin as she traced her lips slowly over his muscular body. Teasing him with her mouth, she worked her magic until he was at the edge too.

"Beth!" he gasped, pulling her to him.

Rolling her over, he covered her with his body, his eyes lost in hers.

"Make love to me, Gareth."

He kissed her lips tenderly as he gladly obliged. Becoming one they moved together, until finally, more shooting stars. They both came together, exploding then melting into each other in a boneless bliss.

A little while later as the night began to cool, Gareth scooped Beth up and carried her to his bedroom. He gazed down at her, sleepy in his arms. She was so small and fragile and yet such a force of life.

Screw the business proposal. This could work, right?

Perhaps he was her happily ever after man, after all?

He wasn't sure what *she* wanted yet. But he wanted her. In his bed. In his arms like this, every night.

CHAPTER 21

----------✶----------

Beth was abandoned and alone in a dusty souk.
As she tried to walk down the market's alleyway, the gap was narrowing, the stalls were closing in on her. Market traders were pestering. Touching her, pushing her to buy things she didn't want. Plastic bags of exotic coloured spices, leather bags and shoes, dangerous cobras that raised their heads out of the baskets the market traders pushed into her face.

She felt suffocated and scared. She screamed for them to move out of her way, to get her out of there. But it was impossible. The souk was a maze and she couldn't escape.

She woke up with a start.

Her heart was thumping.

Where was she?

The dream still lingered in her mind. She'd had it before. Only, it had been a forest. Same thing though. She was lost and abandoned. Trying to get back as the paths closed in.

The duvet was kicked back.

For a moment, a sickening wave washed over her. An irrational echo from the past. Had he left her too?

She heard the tap running in the bathroom and breathed easy.

She rubbed her face.

On the deck, and then again here in his bed. They'd been so good together. For her at least, last night had been the best sex ever. But, they'd crossed a line and there was no going back.

She stretched, now fully awake.

He was her only friend in a new place and she'd turned things super awkward by sleeping with him.

Her Mr-Here-and-Now man.

She humphed.

She needed to play it cool too.

Slipping out of bed, she tied her hair back and put on a big T-shirt of Gareth's that was lying on the floor. The smell of him on it made her heart race.

Then, she snuck downstairs in search of her clothes.

She found them in a big heap by the bi-fold doors.

Quickly dressing, she rolled the rug back tidily in the lounge and took Gareth's clothes upstairs.

He was still in the bathroom, so she sauntered down to the kitchen, filled the kettle and began to make coffee.

Gareth had woken up with Beth curled up into him, her head resting on his chest, fast asleep.

Needing to move, he slid from under her and headed to the bathroom.

As he shaved, the night before replayed in his head and the only thing he could think about now was getting wet with Beth in his new shower.

He'd blown the budget on a wet room with large stone tiles and a powerful shower with body jets.

What better way to start the day?

And this, with Beth, it felt so right.

He stuck a towel around his waist and grabbed another towel for her.

"Beth?"

The bed was neatly made up. His clothes from last night lay folded by his pillow.

Had she got spooked and split?

Hearing the kettle boiling in the kitchen he relaxed.

Then, a second later sheer panic again.

"Yoohoo! Gareth? You up? What happened to you last night?"

That was not what he wanted to hear right now.

The unmistakable voice of his mother, calling from the back door.

Beth heard drawers rattling upstairs as Gareth dressed in record time. He reached the bottom of the stairs at the very moment Ellen strolled through to the main living area, a cake tin in her hands.

She stopped dead in her tracks when she saw Beth standing at the kitchen island.

Smiling angelically at Mrs Morgan, Beth sent up a prayer of thanks that she was dressed. And that she'd cleared all incriminating evidence.

Gareth breezed over to his mother and gave her a peck on the cheek.

He was still slightly out of breath.

"Hi, Mam. Is this for me?"

She gave him the tin and he set it down on the kitchen peninsula.

"A coffee and walnut sponge. Your favourite."

"Thank you."

Beth could smell soap and his aftershave. She was sure his mother could too. Like he'd only just washed and shaved.

"Would you like some tea or coffee, Ellen?"

"*Ooo,* tea please, dear."

She put the two black coffees she'd made to one side.

She felt his mother's eyes fixed on her as she moved around the kitchen, finding the teabags and the milk. And another mug.

"You're back from London, I see?"

She needed to think fast.

"Uh, yeah... Did you try that... *err* pastry after?"

The distraction didn't work, and Ellen didn't respond.

"I've just jogged down to see Gareth for *erm*...a meeting."

She saw his mother's head cock slightly.

"And he's got you making the coffee?"

Gareth cleared his throat.

"Look, there's something we need to tell you and Dad."

Beth tried to catch his eye.

What was coming next?

Beth saw him hastily scanning the room and he threw her a grateful look when he saw that he wouldn't need to be kicking her bikini out of sight.

He drifted over to the sofa and Ellen followed him.

Beth handed them their drinks. Then, grabbing her mug she sat down opposite them on a floor cushion.

She hoped he'd got this covered.

"Mam... me and Beth... well...we got..."

He paused.

Was he going to tell his mother about the marriage? She secretly hoped he would. Get it over and done with.

"Errr... me and Beth got some news recently. In his will, Uncle Evan left us the restaurant and the land. We're having a meeting 'cos we're going to be *business partners*."

Beth watched as Ellen's face changed. She was clearly surprised; shocked even.

"Congratulations... Both of you," she managed, after a moment's silence.

Her enthusiastic tone didn't match her steely expression.

"Neither of us had any idea."

She eyed Beth coldly.

"I bet."

His mother took a drink of her tea.

"Does that mean you're going to be living in Freshwater Bay?"

"Yes. I'm reopening the restaurant. I want to make Evan proud."

Gareth shot Beth a supportive smile.

"And I'm going ahead with the eco-chalet development. Remember, the business plan I showed you and Dad?"

Ellen was sizing them up, Beth could tell.

"How about you come over and tell me and David all about it?" she said finally. "Bring Beth with you for Sunday dinner next week? I'll call you so you'll remember to come this time. Anwen was wondering where you'd got to last night."

Beth saw Gareth's face turn stony.

Ellen quickly drained her tea.

"Well, I'd better get on. I've a feeling that you two have more *business* to discuss."

She hugged her son and turned back to face Beth who was still sat on the floor.

"Nice to see you again, Beth. But, dear... that track's awful stony. You'd be far better jogging in your trainers."

Beth cringed.

Her flip flops were by the door.

The car engine started up and they listened out in silence until she'd gone.

Gareth rubbed his chin and they both burst into laughter.

"We're so busted. The look she gave you when you rushed down the stairs."

He stretched out his hand to help her up off the floor. He sank back down on the sofa and pulled her onto his lap.

"She should've been a detective."

Beth sighed.

"She doesn't like me, I can tell."

Was it because she was an English city girl, like his ex?

"Don't be silly. She was surprised that's all."

He tickled her and Beth squealed.

Gareth was probably right. It must have been a shock to have someone outside the family inheriting the restaurant.

He lifted his hand, gently stroking her face.

"My mother has a heart of gold, but she does like to meddle. That's why it's best to keep this between us for now."

A cold chill ran through her.

"Who the Hell is Anwen?"

Gareth smirked and kissed the tip of her nose.

"Nothing for you to be jealous about. Last night, I got to the farm and she'd invited some random woman to dinner. She was trying to matchmake. I saw what was going on and came back to you."

"I'm glad you did."

Beth screwed up her nose.

"Any other eligible ladies in the parish vying for your affection?"

"Only one. And she's right here."

His lips touched hers.

"Gareth."

She pulled back from him.

"We've totally torn up this business arrangement, you realise that?"

He kissed her again.

"Hmm. I can't keep my hands off you, Beth."

"But we're heading into something we *both* said we didn't want."

He wove her fingers into his as he meditated on that for a moment.

"It doesn't have to be complicated. How about we just explore *this* for a while. What d'you say?"

She didn't disagree. The way he'd touched her. No one had ever come close to making her feel like that before.

"Alright, Mr Morgan. We'd better take that *business* meeting now, then."

He shot her a hungry grin.

"The terms of our agreement Mrs Morgan were changed last night. They now include this."

He slowly stripped off his T-shirt in front of her.

Her eyes widened in mock surprise and she traced her hands over the ridges of his muscular chest.

"I need an update from the previous meeting too please."

She lifted her arms above her head and Gareth obliged, stripping off her T-shirt and bikini top, then pulling out her hairband. Her curls tumbled around her shoulders.

Beth cleared her throat.

"Err, very good progress, Mr Morgan. Well done. Now, matters arising."

Gareth smirked as Beth placed her hand over his shorts.

"Agenda item number one."

She whispered in his ear and he raised an eyebrow.

She nodded.

"But Beth, I don't wanna hurt you."

"You won't. Now fuck me hard, the way I asked you to."

The words ignited the touchpaper and he devoured her with a kiss as they became entangled on the sofa then the floor.

Breathless and sated; sweat beading on their bodies, he gently wrapped himself around her, spooning her as they both fell deliciously back down to earth.

Beth was making them pancakes for breakfast as he came down the stairs from the bathroom.

"You okay?"

"I'm fine."

She smiled at him.

"More than fine... Come. Eat."

He sat on a stool at the peninsular where Beth had put a plate of pancakes and blueberries out.

He couldn't speak right. His brain was still mushed.

"What we did just then..."

He'd never experienced such intensity. Like they were both on fire together. Beth was on another level to anyone he'd been with before.

"That was... that was... "

She shrugged at him cheekily, coming over to where he sat.

"That was... a very productive meeting I'd say, Mr Morgan."

He laughed and drew her close to him, wrapping his arms around her waist.

"And are the new terms acceptable to you, Mrs Morgan?"

She popped a blueberry into his mouth.

"I'm very happy with the terms but I want a new clause added."

"Which is?"

She whispered into his ear, "That you have to do that to me again."

He kissed her tenderly. It was all he could do until his head was ready to listen to what his heart was telling him.

After a late start, Gareth and Beth went up to the restaurant. He was holding good on his word and was eager to make a start on any refurbishments she wanted to make.

By early evening, a large hole in the wall between the kitchen and the restaurant was knocked through.

Gareth's found Beth a little bit too keen on the sledge-hammer. He'd had to rein her in a couple of times, worried that she'd knock out too much wall. She certainly liked to get her hands dirty.

Both of them were covered head to toe in dust.

Their eyes met.

"Time for a clean down?"

The old shower in the flat wasn't a patch on his power jets. But looking at her now, imagining all the things he wanted to do with her, he was sure that it would be plenty hot and steamy.

Hair wet from their long shower and wrapped in towels, they lay on Beth's sofa in the lounge above the restaurant. Arms around each other they looked out at the sea.

They sipped the champagne he'd bought her and talked about the work they needed to do. Gareth was waiting for the public meeting before any development could go ahead with the chalets. The date had been set, but in the meantime there was plenty of building work in the restaurant.

It made sense to split it, he suggested. He would oversee the renovation while she got on with the business side.

She didn't disagree. Today had been fun but she had so much to do. Business plans, banking, interviewing for staff. That was before she even started cooking and getting her menu organised.

"Beth...I've been thinking, it's gonna be real dusty up here while we do the building work... why don't you come stay with me at the boathouse?"

He kissed and grazed her neck teasingly, urging her to say yes.

"Gareth, is that a good idea?"

"Uhh?"

His hand wandered down into her towel, trying to persuade her around.

"I'm serious," she giggled as she moved his hand away.

"You said you didn't want a girlfriend. So, let's keep it simple. Let's just have sex."

Gareth studied her face. He looked like she'd punched him in the gut.

"Beth, I don't care how we label *this*, but I know what I want. And that's you. Not as some drop-in-then-leave kinda thing. I want you with me every night in the boathouse."

She looked searchingly into his dark grey-blue eyes.

It was confusing.

Mr Hot and Cold was sizzling at the moment. But would he cut her down like he had so brutally before?

He'd been badly burned by his marriage, she got that. And she understood how it made him unwilling to commit to a relationship. But staying in the boathouse with him? Would she come to regret that?

"What you gonna tell your parents?"

"Nothing. And I'm not accepting any invitations for dinner."

She shivered as he caressed the back of her neck.

So, she was his secret pleasure. He was still hiding from them, and himself.

She relented.

"Okay. I'll stay with you."

She kissed him coyly.

"But only 'cos you've got a fancy shower."

He grinned wickedly at her and kissed her back.

"And there was me thinking it was because of my huge..."

"Range oven?" she cut across, giggling.

He wrapped her even tighter in his arms.

"That too."

CHAPTER 22

----------*---------

By the end of the following week, the boathouse was stocked with a comprehensive selection of kitchen equipment and store cupboard ingredients to complement Gareth's solitary wooden spoon, fish slice and bottle of sweet chilli sauce.

Neither of them spoke about it. But one by one, the boxes in the apartment were slowly migrating into the boathouse and Beth was fast becoming a big part of Gareth's life.

They'd sent a copy of their marriage certificate to the solicitors and a bottle of champagne had turned up on the restaurant doorstep three days later, together with a note congratulating them.

Gareth hastily took it inside, hoping no-one had seen it by the door.

Each day they rose early and worked at the restaurant. They spent the afternoon exploring the coastline and the night exploring each other.

Most of the dirty construction work was done. And as Gareth tiled the new display kitchen area, his mind kept drifting back to that morning.

They'd been sitting eating breakfast on the deck before they started work. Beth was showing him the pictures she'd pinned of different pottery plates on her phone.

"I'm really liking these stoneware mottled ones."

Gareth pulled a face.

"What?"

"Your food's great. The different pottery? The way it looks? The menu? A lasagne's, a lasagne right?"

Beth chewed her muesli.

"What you doing tonight?"

"Eh?"

"I'm going to show you how it works. You up for it? Try something new?"

What exactly she was going to do, he didn't know. Maybe cook a meal for him and put them on the different plates she was trying?

He was turning into a sad case. He couldn't go more than a few minutes without thinking about her.

It was early evening when Gareth got back from the restaurant, still wondering what Beth's surprise would be. She'd been in the boathouse working on her menus and order lists all afternoon.

He'd half expected the table to be set, pans to be bubbling, candles to be lit. But there was nothing happening in the kitchen. The tops were clear and Beth was shut away in the downstairs bedroom which they were using as an office.

"Hi Gareth," she called out to him. "Hop in the shower and get changed. We're off out."

She was waiting for him as he came downstairs. Sitting on the sofa, the pickup's keys in her hand.

She stood up and he caught his breath.

She was in a patterned halter neck summer dress that slipped silkily over the curves of her breasts and hips.

He suddenly felt under-dressed in his summer shirt and shorts.

"You look fantastic. Do you want me to change?"

"No, you're fine as you are."

She kissed him lightly on the lips and handed him the pickup keys. Turning in front of him to go, the dress revealed the silky cream of her skin as her back lay bare under her long golden curls.

"I've got a better idea. Why don't we stay here and explore this dress?"

She turned playfully and shook her head.

"Tonight, I'm going to teach you the secret of a great menu. *Oh!* And by the way; you're driving."

As they reached the village, she told him to pull over in The Lobster Pot car park.

Of all the places, this would be the last on his list. Only tourists ate here, and usually only the once.

"We could have walked."

She shot him a quirky look.

"Believe me, in a little while you're gonna need the truck."

He got out of the pickup and she waited for him by the harbour wall, beckoning him over.

"Okay. You ready? Lesson number one of a great restaurant is the menu itself."

Beth stepped in front of him and twirled around slowly in her dress.

"It should be tantalising, with just enough adjectives to tempt you further."

She sat on the harbour wall alongside him.

"The slit of a dress, the cut of the material around my breasts, a glimpse of my bare back. It should make you curious."

"I am. Very."

His hungry eyes devoured her. She was enjoying this.

"Good."

She whispered in his ear, "It should make you wonder how it will taste on your tongue."

He turned, staring at her voraciously.

Beth smirked. It didn't take much to fire him up.

She ignored his hound-dog eyes and started walking towards the front entrance.

"Come on, we're going in here."

She gave him a hint of a wicked twinkle as she sat down at a table in the bar lounge and he went to get them a drink.

"Alright, tease. I get it, " he said, handing her a gin and tonic.

"What's next?"

Beth took a sip, then bit her bottom lip. She wasn't sure how he'd react to her next move.

"So, now you see why the menu's got to be good. Lesson number two is the *amuse bouche*. The best restaurants usually give this free. It's an appetiser to entice their customers. To make them want more."

At that Beth got up, and with her small clutch bag disappeared into the toilets.

Gareth was squirming. Marcus, the sleazy landlord had been staring at them from behind the bar.

She emerged a few minutes later and sat down beside him.

She sipped her drink, a little nervously. She could feel her heart beating fast as she pulled her dress down and crossed her legs tightly. She never did stuff like this. But she had to admit, it was thrilling.

"Go on then, what's your amuse bouche?" he asked her.

"You ready?"

She could tell he was worried about what she was going to do next. Gareth and his paranoia about people gossiping about them.

She took her bag from by the side of her and held it towards him under the table.

She snapped the top catch open.

In there, was a bundle of pink lace.

She said under her breath, "I've just taken them off."

"Car... Now. ..Home..."

Beth's face broke into a broad grin as she heard his gruff mumbling. He was struggling to get the words out.

It was working.

She snapped the bag shut and shifted around the table until she was opposite him.

"Fancy another drink?" she suggested breezily.

His face had become stony again. He was trying to keep it together. Teasing him like this was fun.

"You like the amuse bouche, I can tell," she toyed with him co-quettishly. "I think it's time we move to lesson number three."

He raised an eyebrow.

"Lesson number three, the first course is at home."

Gareth sunk the last of his real ale in one gulp.

"Let's go."

Grabbing Beth's hand, he rushed her out the door to the pickup truck, over-revving the engine as he wheel-spinned out of the car park and sped back to the boathouse.

Gareth was wound up like a tiger about to pounce, but Beth was ready for him. She resisted all his attempts to get her up the stairs, and instead made him sit on the stool at the kitchen peninsula.

"As I was saying, lesson number three. For the first course, or starter, we'll be needing this."

Gareth's eyes widened as he saw what she had in her hand.

It was a scarf.

She put it around his eyes, securing it tightly behind his head.

"I've taught you the power of anticipation. Now you need to understand the power of your senses. The first course is all about tantalising your taste buds.."

He heard her walking away.

"Beth?... Where you going?"

Was she going up the stairs?

The blindfold disoriented him. His heart was thumping though. What was she going to do next?

He thought he sensed her around him again.

"Beth, are you there?"

He could feel her presence.

"First, the sense of smell."

Her voice broke the tense silence.

And suddenly, around him, he smelled fragrant, floral notes. It smelled like July. Like the roses growing by the front door. Like when he was a kid, playing in the yard by the farmhouse.

He felt her breath close to him. Something was put by his face. His nose.

Her perfume. He recognised it now. Orange and vanilla, and a little musky.

Tantalising and exciting, his pulse raced and he felt a shot of lust run through him.

He reached out his arms, grabbing into the air.

"Where are you?"

"Take off your shirt."

Her voice was breathy, her tone masterful. And it sent another charge of excitement coursing through him.

He unbuttoned his shirt and slid it off.

Naked to the waist in the blindfold heightened his senses even more. He was vulnerable and exhilarated, not knowing what would happen next.

He heard a zip undoing.

Was that her dress? Oh no, she was moving away.

He heard the fridge door open, then shut.

The pop of a champagne cork pierced the silence like a gunshot, making him jump.

He was alert to every sound. His senses in overdrive.

A crack and a tinkling. Ice being poured into a glass.

She was by him again.

"Touch."

"*Aaahh.*"

He laughed and moaned as an ice cube touched his nipple and then trailed along his abdomen, sending jolts of electricity through him. He could feel his skin prickling.

Pain pleasure.

He wanted her so badly, it hurt.

She moved closer to him. He felt her breath gently by his mouth.

"And now, taste."

She put her lips to his and opened them.

He tasted her hungrily.

And in her mouth, on her tongue were small rounded balls. She moved them onto his and they popped, giving a vivid, rich, slightly sweet and salty taste. Like the sea.

"Caviar," she whispered in his ear.

She put a glass to his mouth and he could feel the bubbles on his lips.

"Drink. What can you taste?"

It was champagne.

He sipped it delicately, something he'd never done before. It amplified all the flavour notes.

"Peach. And almonds."

She moved her hand to his head and untied the scarf.

Gareth was lost for words.

"And finally, after all that. We get to how the dish looks. The presentation on the plate."

Beth was standing there in a deep purple basque, laced down the front. Her hair tumbled like streamers around her shoulders.

"Main course?" he growled.

Unable to take any more of the delicious torture, he bundled her up and carried her, like the caveman she'd called him, up the stairs.

"My turn to cook."

Beth whispered in his ear, "But I still get to do dessert."

CHAPTER 23

----------*---------

"**R**ats!"
Beth couldn't believe it.
She put down her cereal bowl and studied the social media post on Gareth's phone.

"This could sink us before we've even opened. Who'd want to do this to us?"

The post had been shared privately with them by a friend. The picture snapped two rats in the car park with the comment,

'Rats get ready to try out the food at Le Gallois
restaurant, Freshwater Bay.'

Opening up the photo, Gareth could see that the rats had crudely been cut and pasted into the picture. There were still bits of the other picture they'd come from around them.

It was a malicious move by someone who wanted them to fail. But not a professional, they both agreed. If they were, Beth was sure they'd have used roaches. You could buy anything on the internet. And that would've been loads worse to sort out than these poorly cut and pasted rodents.

"So what do we do?" Gareth asked her.

"Fight back."

Gareth reported the post to the online sites to get it taken down. Then he commented on it, exposing the picture as fake.

But it was still out there. And it was reputationally damaging.

Meanwhile, Beth called a pest control company to do a full sweep of the restaurant. Yet more cost.

Malicious reviews happened but she hadn't expected someone to try and kill off her business like this. Who would have most to lose from her restaurant re-opening?

She called Jo. Her friend was the go-to-gal for anything related to social media. She was also a fine investigative journalist. Whilst this wasn't exactly Watergate, she'd be sure to give her some pointers.

Jo took down the details.

"You've done everything you can. Fight fire with fire and post up the pest-control certificate. Make a story and a drama out of the malicious post. It'll turn the news around and get everyone on your side. Any ideas who'd want to close you down?"

Beth rubbed her brow.

"There's the landlord of the local inn, Marcus Wight. It's unlikely that it's him, though. The place's really shabby and he doesn't look that bothered about the business."

"Okay... Well, I'll do a few searches too," Jo confirmed. "I'll find out more about it and get back to you."

Beth gave Jo Gareth's number too.

"Gareth's my business partner. I might be difficult to get hold of once the restaurant gets going. If you need to contact me urgently try his number."

She heard Jo's snigger at the other end of the line.

"Is this the same *business partner* who was your builder too?"

Flummoxed, Beth struggled to respond. Nothing got past Jo Mack.

When Beth told Ariana quietly about her new arrangement with Gareth, she squealed with delight, turning Beth's cheeks scarlet as customers in the coffee shop turned around.

She'd wanted to keep it secret but she trusted Ariana, and people had started seeing Beth and Gareth together, out and about or in the pub. It was hardly news, except maybe to his family.

She didn't have a label for what it was they had. She'd been thinking about that a lot recently.

She wanted to be with him and it hurt when she thought that it might all end. But, the reality was that nothing had been said between them about their relationship since they first were together. Beth secretly couldn't help but worry that perhaps sex was all there was to it.

They'd taken a trip into town, twenty miles away. Beth needed to meet suppliers and Ariana had told her that she could do with a change of scene too.

Ariana loved Freshwater Bay, and wouldn't ever want to move away. But every now and then she had to get out. A city, she didn't care which one. But she needed its buzzing bars, shops and galleries like a fix.

Beth got that completely. The quietness of Freshwater Bay after London was quite a culture shock for her too. Not that she'd had much time to think about that.

Ariana reminded Beth of some of her artistic London friends. She was a bit 'out there.' And right at that moment, she'd put down her cappuccino and was holding Beth's hand, staring at the ring she'd designed and made as if it had special powers.

"Ariana, I'm not sure about this ring stuff. But I'm in a really happy place right now with Gareth. It's a bit unconventional but it's good."

"Said it'd bring you hot sex, girl."

Beth turned fifty more shades of red.

"And judging by your face, I'm not wrong."

She diverted the conversation quickly.

"What about you? Are you seeing anyone?"

"No."

Ariana let go of Beth's hand and turned her attention back to her coffee. She stirred it pensively with her teaspoon, scooping up some chocolate dusted froth.

"I'm talking to a guy... In the States."

"Gareth's brother's in LA. It's not him is it?"

Ariana's face wrinkled up like she'd tasted a lemon.

"Rhys Morgan? *Ugh!* No. That was over when I was a kid. He's such an arrogant, conceited, shallow, manipulative, egotistical, two-faced slimeball."

Beth rolled her eyes and laughed out loud.

"Okay... I take it you're not a fan, then?"

"That's an understatement. You got the nice one, honey. Gareth's a genuine guy. Rhys, on the other hand, is a total shit. Thankfully, he never comes home."

"How did you two split?"

"Let's just say he was too tied up to treat me the way I deserved," she answered cryptically.

Beth dropped it. Ariana's face told her that she wasn't getting any more information.

"So, who is he? This guy in America?"

Ariana's face lit up.

"Oh, ya know, just someone I chat to online. He handles my art deals out there. He does sales on this website he's got. He's very talented. And I can't deny that there's a connection between us."

"What's his name?"

"His username's Lucentio. He calls himself Luc. I think he might be of Italian descent, like me. Not sure, though. We have a rule that we don't discuss personal details," she admitted candidly.

"He... he could be a thirty stone, married crackhead with eight kids. It's just chat. No cameras. No biography. Nothing that gets in the way of our minds connecting."

"And one day, might you guys meet up for real?"

She bit her lower lip.

"I have thought about that, but I've got this image of him in my head, and I'm scared in case I'm disappointed. So, in the meantime, we chat, talk about books, films, life. Shit like that."

"He could be a catfish?"

Beth had heard about men sparking up friendships online and then conning women out of money.

"No. He's never asked for anything. It's him who pays me and gets me the art sales. Luc's cultured. He reads a lot. He's like my soul mate."

Beth smiled kindly at her friend. She sounded a little lonely.

With his keen architect's eye, Gareth saw that the restaurant needed more complexity to the space, and he was busy raising the floor behind the bar when his phone rang.

Madog was stuck for a sitter. Ellen and David were at the agricultural show all day and a cow was calving.

He told Madog he'd gladly help. Beth would be back soon and it would be fun having little Jake.

When Gareth got to the boathouse, carrying Jake in his car seat, Beth was already back from her trip to town.

Jake was awake and Gareth gently got him out of the car seat. Cradling him in his arms, he took him inside.

"Hey buddy, let's see what your Auntie Beth's doing?"

"Auntie Beth?" she uttered hearing him come in. "Is that Jake?... Hello, little man."

She cooed around the baby.

"You haven't even told your mother I'm living here, so I hardly think I've acquired Auntie status yet."

Gareth took that stinger on the chin. She had a point.

"What you up to?"

The kitchen peninsular was littered with scribbled sheets of paper, full of crossings out. She gathered them up and scrunched them into a ball.

"I'm struggling. I've been wracking my brains to find a signature dish that uses local ingredients. But the ideas aren't flowing today."

"I'll take you out on the boat. Get some seafood. Razor clams, mussels, crabs, crayfish, cockles."

She smiled at him appreciatively.

"Yum. Thank you."

She stretched up and kissed him.

Taking Jake into her arms, she blew on his little belly, making him giggle.

Later, Beth sat on a floor cushion with a cup of tea watching Gareth with Jake. She felt an all-consuming, aching pang of tenderness towards him as he fed a sleepy Jake his bottle of milk. He was such a natural with him.

But what did Gareth want from his life, she wondered?

And how did *she* fit into it?

She'd been irritated when he'd called her Auntie Beth. And she'd meant what she said. They were living together in all but name.

And the name was beginning to matter.

She wasn't even his girlfriend.

He hadn't manned up yet and told his parents. Was he ashamed of their relationship?

And what if he grew tired of her?

She'd got it so badly wrong before. Perhaps she had this time too?

She needed to ease her mind.

Leaving Gareth to settle Jake to sleep, she changed into her swimsuit and plunged from the deck into the sea.

Gareth watched Beth as she went out for a swim. The image of her that day still an echo in his mind.

Jake was now asleep in his arms. His mouth was open and the empty rubber teat of the bottle rested on his little cheek.

He needed winding and Gareth lifted him carefully to his shoulder to rub his back, hoping that Jake wouldn't wake up too much or be sick on his shoulder.

He'd like a child one day with Beth.

With Beth.

But, what did she even think about kids? He had no idea.

The sex was fantastic but he was at a loss to understand what was going on in her head. They never talked about their relationship or a future together. Both of them avoided it.

Her right-here-right-now-guy. He'd given himself that label. But, there was no getting around it, whatever he called what they had together, he was in a full-on relationship with this beautiful, amazing woman. And he'd never been happier.

He'd never felt as close to anyone else. And yet, in so many ways she was still a stranger to him.

He needed time alone with her, away from the restaurant.

Just the two of them. On the boat.

CHAPTER 24

----------✳---------

"What? And now you're living with him?"

Jo was on Facetime with Beth and she wasn't at all impressed by her friend's situation.

Beth had told her everything. Gareth, the business arrangement they'd made, the wedding...

And in return, her so-called 'friend', the award-winning journalist, was hurling every single problem that she could possibly think of at her as if she were interrogating a corrupt politician on a news programme.

"Beth, what *were* you thinking of? If you build a successful restaurant, he'd be entitled to half of it."

"I could do the same with his development project."

"Did you get any background checks on him before you got hitched? He could be a criminal for all you know."

"Jo, he's got an honest face. He thought *I* was the con-artist, trying to swindle Evan."

"And you're together, right? Living with him? And what did you say, you've got some kind of friends with benefits arrangement?"

"Jo, it's not like that. It's fun. He makes me happy."

"For *now*, maybe. But has he shown you any commitment at all? How d'you know he's not playing you, Beth?"

Jo was worried for her, she said. She kept banging on about how

Beth had got herself into a situation where she was submissive to a man she barely knew. She'd moved into his house with no indication that he even cared for her, she vented. And it sounded to Jo like Gareth was calling all the shots.

"I had my eyes open going into this, Jo. He told me from the off that he couldn't offer me a relationship."

"But, honey, you're living together! That sounds like a relationship to me."

"It's not. Because it's not official. His parents don't know."

"You think?"

"Has he told you he loves you yet?"

Beth went quiet, then changed the subject.

"Ratgate's over. Did you find anything out about Marcus?"

"Nothing of any interest, " Jo answered, taking the hint that Beth's love life was not up for any more debate. "He's had a couple of scrapes with the law and has been running pubs before this one, mainly up North. The Lobster Pot's owned by a company called Penfroz Holdings. That's about it, sorry."

"Well, at least the social media post has gone. And I've had hundreds of likes on my new restaurant page."

Jo's face softened as she looked directly down the camera at her friend.

"Listen, Beth. I'm sorry about what I said about you and Gareth. I'm just worried for you, that's all. You both need to start talking to each other. This fuckbuddy arrangement won't work out long-term. Not when you're so obviously in love with him."

"Jo! I'm not..."

She started to protest and then stopped. There was no fooling Jo. She'd caught feels for Gareth.

She loved him.

And when this all ended, it was going to hurt like Hell.

Beth had never been on a sailboat before and was intrigued and confused by the workings of the jib and the mainsail.

With Gareth at the helm, tacking the boat downwind and directing course, they sailed out into the bay and over to one of the islands that faced the boathouse.

Beth decided that it was best to stay clear of the action. She sat on the deck and watched the shoreline get smaller and smaller as they moved away from the mainland.

As they neared their chosen island shore, they weighed anchor and waded onto the beach.

When Gareth had suggested an overnight trip on the boat, Beth had jumped at the chance. It would be difficult to have breaks once the restaurant was opened.

And this felt like a holiday. They swam and sunbathed, then meandered around the rock pools on the shoreline. They scrambled over the rocky promontory and watched a small colony of seals play in the waves and then waddle up to their island beach in the hot July sun.

On their way back to the boat, they collected mussels into a bucket for dinner.

Gareth pointed to a rock.

"See that over there? We eat it. It's laver seaweed."

They waded together through the tide over to the rock. It was covered in a glossy, black mat of seaweed which hung off the sides like the rock was having a bad hair day.

Beth was sceptical. It didn't look edible.

"What's it taste like?"

Gareth smirked.

"Ah, I've sparked your interest now. It's Welshman's caviar, that is. Spinachy and salty."

"How'd you…"

"Cook it? You boil it for hours and then purée. Roll it in oatmeal and fry it up with bacon and cockles for breakfast."

"Yum. Can we get some for me to try?"

"Sure."

She tried to pull the seaweed off the rock, but fell backwards into the water. It wasn't going to submit to her charms that easily. Not when it could withstand the strength of force ten gales in the Irish Sea.

She heard Gareth chuckling behind her.

"Stop. You'll damage the plant if you pull, and then it won't grow back. We need to cut it with scissors."

They returned to the boat and then, armed with scissors they gathered a bucket load of the seaweed.

Purée, caviar? Tastes of the sea?

The ideas were starting to form. She'd made squid ink tuiles before. They were black wafers with latticed holes just like a piece of coral and they made a dramatic feature on the plate, as well as adding texture and a salty sea flavour. Plus, they'd store well.

What if she made laverbread tuiles?

Brilliant. She was itching to try it out as soon as she got back to shore.

As the afternoon rolled into the evening, they started to get hungry. Back on board, Gareth fished while Beth fried down the chopped onion contentedly in the tiny galley kitchen below deck. And as she did most days, she sent Evan a silent prayer of thanks.

She made them moules mariniere. And with the setting sun out west, they sat on the deck emptying the freshly harvested mussel shells into their mouths and dipping their homemade bread into the white wine sauce.

Gareth gazed out to the islands and back to Beth, her hair glistening in the golden sunlight.

She looked at him curiously as he stared at her.

"What?"

"That's how I saw you first."

"What? With sauce dribbling down my chin?"

"No. Like this. With the evening sun shining on you, turning your hair into strands of gold. That's how I noticed you. I thought to myself, she's the most beautiful girl, I've ever seen."

Beth gazed at him and smiled.

"I had my eye on you too. I was checking you out when you got out of your kayak."

"You weren't?"

"Uh-huh. I was."

"I sat all night in The Lobster Pot hoping you'd come down the stairs."

She kicked out her legs and stretched back.

"This place is heaven, Gareth."

"Beth?"

"Hmm?"

He looked searchingly into her eyes and her heart thumped hoping he'd say the words she longed to hear.

"Uhh... you look cold."

The sun had set and the air was getting chilly.

She smiled weakly as Gareth took her hand and led her down to the bedroom below deck.

Taking her in his arms they made love tenderly as the softly lilting waves rocked underneath them.

As Beth lay in his arms, her eyes closed, the doubts and uncertainty she'd been fighting back welled up within her again.

The golden sunset, the perfect day. When would he *ever* tell her that he loved her?

Or, was the hard truth that he didn't?

Gareth Morgan held her fragile heart in his hands.

The man was a classic commitment phobe. He'd told her that from the start. She should never have expected more.

He'd laughed as he watched her getting up out of the water, her shorts soaked through. Messing about in the waves, sunbathing, exploring the island; it had been such a wonderful day.

Gareth lay in the cramped bed with Beth in his arms. He couldn't remember a time when he'd been happier.

He loved her with all his heart. There was no doubt about that.

But, would telling her spook her?

He'd nearly said it when they watched the sunset. But he'd bottled it. She was the one who'd made it clear that she didn't want labels.

And what if she didn't love him?

He couldn't bear the thought of messing this up. Whatever *this* was, he wanted it to last.

"Rwyn dy garu di, Beth."

Gareth whispered the Welsh words into Beth's hair as she slept. He'd told her he loved her.

And he did.

CHAPTER 25

----------✳---------

F reshwater Bay village hall was packed out for the public meeting about Gareth's proposed development. Locals and other interested parties sat on plastic seats set
out in rows.

There was a buzz in the room as people greeted one another,
and there was much discussion and curiosity about what this
local lad, the architect who'd come back to Freshwater Bay was
planning to do.

Gareth cut a lonely figure. He stood at the front of the hall to
the side of a temporary projector screen, on which he was going
to show an animated film of the development.

He looked professional and confident in his well-cut navy suit,
Beth thought proudly. She'd recognised it when he put it on that
evening. It was the suit he'd worn on their wedding day.

Of the sea of faces in front of Gareth, most were familiar and
friendly. There were a few at the front he'd not seen before. One
or two stared at him, hard-faced and solemn.

His parents were there, chatting to neighbours and relatives.
Ariana had caught his eye and given him a thumbs up. At the
back of the hall, he saw Beth sitting discreetly out of view but
taking in all of the crowd.

He'd overheard a couple of whispers already about them. He heard one say that she was Gareth's new girlfriend, from London. Another talked about the restaurant re-opening soon. And that she'd bought it. He couldn't focus on any of that now.

The meeting time had slipped by five minutes. He had one shot at selling his vision. He nodded to a friend at the back who dimmed the lights.

Gareth took a deep breath and began the greatest pitch of his life.

He spoke passionately for a good twenty minutes about his love of the area, his environmental credentials and his past experiences as an architect, particularly on sustainable building.

He explained the sensitive development, the features of the build and elaborated on the economic and community benefits, outlining his proposal for the permanent residences.

The audience listened politely and watched the video. At the end of the presentation most of the audience clapped.

A middle-aged man in a checked shirt and jeans stood up. Tommy Shop; he owned the village's convenience store.

"Gareth, I say that this is exactly what we need in Freshwater Bay. It'll bring money into the village and it'll mean our kids can have somewhere they can afford to live."

A single clap and then a smattering of applause from around the room.

A heckler in favour added, "And it'll mean the school'll stay open."

This time more people clapped. The village school was a sensitive issue.

Three more locals expressed support for the development.

One lady then raised concerns about the seabirds and their habitat.

Gareth was straight on it. He gave her a knowledgeable response explaining the zero impact of the build as it was away from the nesting grounds, which would be fenced off.

The mood music was positive and Gareth was heartened. He'd anticipated a rough ride. From his previous architect experi-

175

ences, these meetings were usually incredibly tough.

There was quiet in the audience and Gareth moved to draw the meeting to a close.

Just then, at the front, a rotund man dressed in an expensive tweed jacket and cravat stood up.

Locals in the crowd whispered to each other. They'd never seen the man before. One said that he had a limousine outside, with a driver.

"*I* have an objection."

The man stood up and half faced the audience, as if he was setting himself in competition with Gareth to win them over.

"We bought our properties in this area based on its remoteness. We will be objecting based on the effect that this will have on our portfolio and the increased traffic on the harbour front. I'll be engaging my lawyers on this in the morning."

Gareth was momentarily floored by the threat of a legal challenge.

"Well, erm... the traffic, it won't be going through the harbour past your cottages, Sir. Your property values shouldn't be affected by the development and local people do need tourism for jobs, so we can all afford to live in Freshwater Bay."

The audience was mumbling again. So, this was the man who owned all the fishing cottages that were now holiday homes, empty much of the year. Gareth was struggling to keep a lid on the crowd.

At the back, he saw a movement. Beth had stood up. No-one paid much attention to her at first.

She gestured to him. Could she speak?

He wasn't sure it was a good idea, but he nodded and she started making her way down the aisle.

He heard the whispering begin again. He cringed as he heard his name and the boathouse mentioned. They'd not gone unnoticed.

Beth reached the front of the aisle and stood by Gareth, facing square on to the cantankerous gent in the front who had just spoken.

Beth scanned the crowd and then focussed on him, giving him a dazzling smile.

He, in return, looked confused and recalcitrant.

"Err.. good evening ladies and gentlemen. My name's Beth and I'm the new co-owner of Le Gallois. The restaurant and the eco-chalet development are part of a package. And that package is *us*."

She gestured at herself and Gareth.

Gareth glanced sideways at her. Was she telling everyone that they were together?

What was his family going to say about this? The gossip would be never-ending.

He wavered a little, mortified at the attention that this would bring him.

"I promise you that our restaurant and the developments alongside it will mean that your property investment, Mr Fawksley-Brown, will only appreciate in value."

Gareth was stunned.

She knew him.

She carried on, addressing the large gentleman directly.

"Lovely to see you again, by the way.... As one of my *best* and most *valued* customers at La Vie en Rose in London, you've enjoyed my food... quite a few times, if I remember rightly."

The gentleman smiled.

A couple of people in the audience sniggered unkindly.

"So... I'm sure that you agree then, Sir, that your holiday lettings will receive a significant boost from the draw of a prestigious restaurant on their doorstep."

His face was impenetrably blank.

She addressed the crowd directly again.

"Not only that, but my restaurant will be a training centre too."

"With rats."

A loudly whispered heckle from a few seats back.

That made sense now.

Gareth watched as the landlord of the Lobster Pot rocked back on his chair.

Beth jumped on it and stared directly at the heckler.

"No. No rats, Marcus, I can assure you. Never were. I am glad for your concern though, *and* your posts."

People began chattering and chairs scraped as some of the audience turned to look at the red-faced publican.

"As I was saying," she began again loudly.

The crowd hushed.

"As I was saying, the restaurant will train staff to have the best skills in hospitality so that they can work here, or anywhere else in the world. I hope that you will all support us."

Beth looked tentatively at the audience and at Mr Fawksley-Brown.

The hall was silent.

Then, three people, ten more, then most of the audience were clapping.

Bethan beamed.

Mr Fawksley-Brown got up too and shook her hand.

"I'll be in touch."

He promptly turned and walked out of the hall.

Beth stood alongside him as he thanked the officers from the Planning Department for attending. They could see no real issues emerging from the meeting, unless there were written objections. They promised they would let Gareth know of their decision after the end of the consultation period and the council planning meeting.

"Hey? Beth the Chef?"

A parent of a teenage boy wanted to find out more about possible apprenticeships.

She told the father to get his son to call up at the restaurant and then edged her way back through the people towards Gareth who was in front of her with his back turned.

He was in mid-conversation with his parents.

And every word she overheard stabbed her like a skewer right through the heart.

"No. I told you. We're purely business partners."

"But, what about all the gossip?" Ellen asked.

"There's nothing going on, Mam. You know what people 'round here are like."

Gareth grinned as she stood beside him.

"Beth the Chef, eh?"

Beth cast her eyes to the floor.

Taking a deep breath, she set her face and smiled sweetly at him. Even though inside her heart was breaking.

Making her excuses, she'd left them to it and had gone back to the boathouse, alone.

It was late now.

Standing on the boathouse deck, the islands were dark indigo shadows in the moonlit night.

Gareth had gone to The Lobster Pot with his friends.

Despite the warm air around her, Beth felt a cold chill.

Gareth didn't love her.

She'd presumed that by living in the boathouse with him they'd slide seamlessly into a life together.

The lie to his parents was the slap in the face she needed.

She was just his fuckbuddy after all.

His business terms had been crystal clear. It was her who'd messed it all up by falling in love.

They'd had fun together. They were great mates. But as he'd said to her those few weeks ago, he wasn't capable of committing to a relationship.

Should she just carry on taking what he was prepared to give her?

Could she live like that, knowing he didn't love her?

The restaurant sat in oppressive blackness at the top of the cliff above her head. What price was she prepared to pay for her dream?

CHAPTER 26

----------✳---------

Beth buried herself in work. The restaurant refurbishment was very nearly completed and she hoped to be open by the summer school holidays. It was better keeping her mind on the tasks in hand. If she agonised over their relationship she'd get weepy. Hormonal even.

It was an odd feeling, like a cloud slowly closing around her. Suffocating her. A couple of times she'd gone into the storeroom at the back of the restaurant kitchen and had a little cry.

Another thing had been bothering her too. A couple of days after the public consultation meeting she'd received a letter. She'd kept it in her menu folder as she agonised over whether to tell Gareth.

In the end, she called Jo.

"But it's from Penfroz Holdings," she explained as Jo read over a scan of the letter.

"Perhaps they've had their eye on the place and want to consolidate their portfolio? The Lobster Pot and your restaurant?" Jo suggested. "Bloody Hell, Beth. A million quid. Think what you could do with that."

"I'm not selling. That's why I'm not saying a word to Gareth about it."

"Listen, Beth. I'll have a dig around into Penfroz for you. How about that?"

"You sure?"

"Yeah. See who you're dealing with."

"How are things with you and Gareth?"

Beth shrugged sadly at the screen.

"You were right. I've made a massive mistake. I really love him, Jo. But I'm not sure he's on the same page as me."

A tear welled up. She was so weepy these days.

"Hang on in there, Beth. And for God's sake talk to him. It's no good letting it eat you up like this."

Beth sniffed.

"You're right. I will."

Jo ended the call.

A wave of sadness overwhelmed her again.

Talk to him. Easier said than done. If she did tell him that she loved him, would he run scared and end it?

Gareth felt the change in Beth. It was since the meeting. Something had happened between them, but he wasn't sure what it was.

He paddled through the waves trying to get his head straight about it.

Over the last week, she'd been gone by the time he woke up and then she'd come home really late, exhausted. They'd been eating at different times, and for the last few nights she'd pecked him on the cheek and rolled over to sleep.

He was worried about her. He was worried about what was happening to them. He'd seen her busy before, when she was chatting online to him in London and when they'd been working on this project. This was different. It was like she was avoiding him.

What had he done?

Whatever it was, he needed to sort it. Tell her he wanted her in his life, for her to be his girlfriend.

That sounded odd. She was already his wife. She'd understand what he meant.

He should have told his parents in the meeting and got it over and done with. But he was nervous about putting her on the spot, like that. What if she wasn't cool with it, too?

He was so proud of her. The way she stood up to that jerk in the planning meeting. And her vision for the restaurant. He wanted the world to know that they were together.

He gathered his courage as he paddled. He'd find a time when she wasn't distracted. Go somewhere quiet where they could sit down together and talk this through.

The restaurant refurbishment was complete. The dining area walls were now a soft grey and sage, offset by large elaborate golden gilt-framed mirrors above the booths that Ariana had created for them.

The bar had been transformed into a dramatic carved cabinet jammed with interestingly shaped spirit bottles. Harry Hops had come good and fitted the latest water dripping pumps. Multilevel areas behind the bar broke up the space.

Beth had created a cocktail and gin menu which used all the tricks of the trade, from fruit syrups to crushed and even dry ice.

Her menus were completed. She was now ready for some honest feedback. She set up a chef's table in the back kitchen and invited Gareth for lunch.

After lunch, they'd talk.

The time felt right. It was the start of her new venture. Make or break. Like them.

Gareth was a little edgy when he came into the kitchen. He must have been picking up on her vibes. She felt bad; she'd hardly said two words to him that morning.

She pecked him on the cheek and he sat down at the table.

"You'll have to excuse me while I get the dishes out."

She left him sitting alone.

A few minutes later, she set a mottled-glazed earthenware

bowl in front of him. In the centre were three seared scallops on a bed of pea purée. They'd been dusted with cockles and pea shoots, and a laverbread tuile jutted out from the centre. A delicate coral-like wafer.

"Well? Be honest with me, Gareth. Do you like it? Is it good enough?"

She nervously held her breath as he chewed it carefully.

"Beth, this tastes amazing. It tastes like home. Like here."

That was all she needed.

"It would be better if I was wearing a blindfold," he winked.

She nudged him playfully in the back with her elbow as she took his plate away.

The next dish was a crab and grapefruit salad that was cleansing and light.

Afterwards, a sea bass dish with buttery carrots and sweet, roasted, golden beetroot in a rich garlic, ginger and miso sauce. And then, herb-crusted, roasted lamb chops with hazelnuts and dijon mustard.

He was no expert, he told her but they all tasted fantastic. And each one, so different.

"Beth, honey. I can't handle any more food. I'd be stoked if I ordered any of those dishes."

She spared him the dessert and pulled up a chair to sit opposite him.

She still had a few more tweaks with the dishes. She was never a hundred percent happy, but she was pleased. She just hoped that her customers and food critics would be as generous in their praise.

The lamb dish was still on the table. She should be hungry, she'd not eaten herself. But cooking all morning had made her feel nauseous.

She put that out of her mind. They needed to talk. And now was as good a time as any.

"Gareth? Now the restaurant's done, we need to discuss what's next."

His face had turned flinty and her stomach churned again.

"Yeah. I had a letter this morning. From the Planning Office. There are objections registered for the development."

"Mr Fawksley-Brown?"

"Yes. Him. But there's been a sighting of some rare moth on the site as well. It's a protected species. It's the worst possible outcome."

"Why?"

Gareth rubbed his eyes and breathed out.

"They'll need to do studies and tests on the environment. Set up, I don't know, moth traps and stuff. It could take months. Years, even."

He looked at her, deflated.

"It's a professional wrecking job, Beth. Someone's out to make the development fail. It happened to one of my clients."

"What did you advise?"

"To sell up. The legal fees alone'll cost thousands."

She moved her stool over towards him and put her arm around him. He leaned his head against her shoulder and she felt him breathing heavily as they came together.

She held his face in her hands and brought her lips to his.

"It's alright. We'll work through this."

He kissed her back. It felt so good.

His eyes met hers as they ended the kiss.

"Beth. What's up? You've not been yourself for a couple of weeks. I'm worried. Tell me. Please."

She screwed her nose, deciding what to say. He'd got enough going on with her ratcheting it up about their relationship.

"I've been stressed, that's all. With the restaurant."

"Sure?"

"I'm fine. Honestly."

She bit her lip.

"Now, how about you give me a hand clearing these."

She winked at him.

"You'll be after a job washing up here if this development's canned."

He stacked the plates into a pile.

"I still think we need some time together."

He stared at her quizzically.

"I wanna fly something else by you. Fancy a paddle later, over to the island?"

She shot him a smile.

"Sounds good."

"And then, Mrs Morgan. Since you've made me all this delicious food, I intend to spoil you tonight."

"And exactly how do you intend to do that?"

"How about a hot shower after our paddle, then a bottle of wine and an early night?"

Beth stretched her arms around his neck and reached up to kiss him.

"I need to cook for you more often."

During the lunch, he'd missed a thousand opportunities. But she'd been so busy bringing food out, and then so anxious as she waited for his feedback.

She focussed on the tiniest of details. Were the nasturtiums in the crab salad too much? Would people eat laverbread as a tuile? He couldn't shift the conversation to their relationship.

So he'd bottled it, again.

Then he'd told her about the project. And asking her straight after wouldn't have been right, either. He didn't want her to feel sorry for him when he told her how much he loved her.

So, paddling out to the island was the best plan he had. Then, they'd sit together on the beach and they'd talk. Properly.

He loved Beth. And there was nothing more to be said. He wanted her in his life forever.

But it couldn't go on like it was. Not even as his girlfriend.

He was her husband and Beth was his wife. And they should be together with the whole world knowing it.

He'd ask her to marry him again. Face to face, this time.

And they could renew their vows. In front of the whole village,

if she wanted.
  He was definitely going to ask her.
  When they got to the island.

CHAPTER 27

----------*---------

The water was calm and the sun glistened onto the surface, making it sparkle. They'd developed a good steady rhythm now that they'd been kayaking together a fair bit.

There was a dolphin pod out in the bay and they'd been watching it as they paddled. Having cleared the headland, they'd travelled about a third of the way to the islands and reached the open sea.

In the rear of the kayak, Gareth was on autopilot. He was busy rehearsing the words in his head. It was the perfect place to ask her. He hoped she'd agree.

Out of nowhere, the kayak suddenly tipped sideways, wobbling dangerously.

He struggled to steady them.

"Woah!"

Beth's oar had hit the water flat.

He could see that she was doubled forward, and she was writhing in pain.

"*Argh!*"

She tried to pull her knees up and the kayak wobbled dangerously again.

Gareth worked hard to steady it and stop them from tipping into the sea.

"*Beth!* You alright?"

"*Oww.*"

She was in acute pain. It sounded serious.

"What's wrong? Try not to move, hun. You'll tip the kayak and we'll be in trouble."

From behind her, he couldn't see her face.

"I think it might be my appendix. We need to get back," she groaned.

He was filled with panic but he couldn't show it. This was a dangerous situation for them both. They were in the middle of the open waters.

Grimly, he turned the kayak and started to paddle back towards the bay.

It was hard going.

His stomach clenched. The land was quite far away and double kayaks weren't designed for passengers. He was constantly afraid they'd tip, and he couldn't risk a capsize.

She'd already vomited twice and the jolts of pain were getting worse. He needed her help if they were going to get to land soon.

"Beth, we've got no choice. You have to paddle with me. Keep your paddle with mine. Left... Right... Left... Right..."

She responded, working with him as he called out.

"Great. Keep going, focus on the strokes and shout if you need to rest."

Gareth pushed hard. The pain wasn't going away. She was getting them regularly in pulses.

Thankfully, after thirty minutes or so, they finally reached the boathouse where Gareth steadied the kayak to help her out.

"Beth, I'm taking you to hospital."

She got out of the kayak and staggered onto the slipway, overcome again by a wave of dizzying pain. She wretched into the sea as he pulled the kayak out of the water.

Carrying Beth up to the boathouse in his arms, he set her to lean against the pickup while he grabbed his keys.

He quickly threw together a bag of her things. He couldn't afford to wait for an ambulance. He was driving her straight to the Accident and Emergency Unit of the hospital twenty miles away.

Sitting in the passenger seat, Beth writhed in pain, silently enduring the agony, trying to be brave. She tried deep breathing but she was sure her appendix was bursting.

"Hang on in there. We'll be there soon."

Gareth pushed harder on the accelerator and prayed.

Please God, make the pain go away. Let her be okay.

He arrived at the A&E entrance alongside a row of ambulances and helped her out of the cab.

Two paramedics were passing, taking an elderly patient in on a trolley. Taking one look at Beth, one of them rushed to help. He did a quick assessment, grabbed a wheelchair and whisked her inside at speed, telling Gareth to park up and then join them.

The hospital was busy. It took a while to find a space. And when Gareth reached the entrance he found a long queue of people waiting to register and a room full of people sitting in rows waiting to be seen.

He couldn't wait in line. There wasn't time.

People grumbled as Gareth raced past the queue up to the window hatch and asked the receptionist if she'd seen someone newly admitted being wheeled in.

She shook her head.

Gareth moved away from the window and scanned the waiting area. Where had she gone?

He started asking random people. Anyone who might have seen Beth being wheeled in.

"'Scuse me... Sir!... I saw her."

Raising his hand to him, an elderly gentleman sitting in the corner of the waiting area called him over.

"She was taken that way."

The area said authorised personnel only.

He thanked the man and jogged through to the treatment area. Where was she?

He grabbed the attention of a busy-looking nurse.

"I'm looking for Beth Morgan. A young blonde lady in a wheelchair. She's just come in with a paramedic."

The nurse pointed to a closed curtain.

"In there, having tests. Can I ask what your relationship to the patient is, please?"

"I'm her husband."

Beth heard Gareth and a female voice as she drifted back into consciousness.

"She fainted but she's coming round now. We're doing some tests. Acute abdominal pain, vomiting, fainting. Could be a number of things."

She could feel that she was strapped to a monitor.

And that Gareth was sitting with her. She felt his hand holding hers. She squeezed it, trying to reassure him.

"What happened there?" she said shakily.

"You fainted. They're doing tests."

"Ahh!"

Gareth held her hand tightly as another jolt of pain shot through her. It was worse than any cramps she'd ever experienced. The nurses couldn't give her anything for it in case she needed surgery.

A doctor holding a clipboard came through the curtains. She was studying the notes.

"Beth, can I ask you, when did you last have a period?"

Beth thought back. She couldn't remember. It was a while ago.

"*Uh... May?*"

The doctor nodded.

"Your hormones are raised. We need to do a scan."

"What does that mean? I've got a coil."

Gareth was trying to keep up. Was she pregnant?

The doctor calmed her.

"Let's not jump the gun. Let's see what's going on first."

Beth was taken in a wheelchair to the ultrasound room with Gareth at her side and prepared for her scan.

The doctor's face was grim as she examined the grainy black

and white images on the large screen in front of her. She studied the screen from all angles as she moved the probe around Beth's uterus.

Something wasn't right.

"I'm sorry, Beth. It's an ectopic pregnancy and not viable. Judging by the scan, it's six to seven weeks. We need to get you into surgery. It'll be keyhole but you'll need a general anaesthetic. And I have to tell you, we may need to remove the fallopian tube."

Another miscarriage. Beth felt herself getting distressed as tears began to well up.

Gareth gripped her hand in silence, his face set like granite. Impenetrable.

"Will I be able to have children?"

The doctor laid her hand on Beth's shoulder.

"You're jumping the gun again, Beth."

"Let's take this one step at a time."

Beth was taken back to the treatment area and prepared for surgery by a nurse as Gareth sat on a plastic chair at her bedside.

He felt helpless. Pathetic. Totally unable to support her with either the physical or emotional pain she was going through.

Another tear rolled down her cheek and she batted it away.

"I'm sorry, Gareth. If you want to leave, I'll understand."

He studied her face.

"I'm not going anywhere. We'll get through this together, cariad. I promise."

She didn't understand Welsh, but it felt right. It was the first time he'd called her his love.

He leaned over and kissed her lovingly on the lips.

"Beth, you mean the world to me."

She nodded absently and squeezed his hand.

"These last few weeks have changed my life. What we've had together, it's been amazing. I never thought that I'd ever... But you, you're everything to me. What I mean to say Beth is that I..."

A nurse pulled back the curtains.

"We're ready for you now."

"I'm scared, Gareth."

He kissed her forehead.

"Everything'll be fine, cariad."

The anaesthetist and an orderly came in to take her.

"I'm Adam and I'm going to be looking after you."

He motioned to her finger.

"That ring'll have to come off."

She pressed it into Gareth's hand.

Adam signalled to the orderly and they began to roll her away.

"We'll take good care of your wife. Don't worry."

She disappeared through a set of double doors.

Gareth was dazed.

His eyes fixed on the doors.

"Mr Morgan?"

A nurse directed him to an empty waiting room where he sat on an uncomfortable plastic chair.

Gazing at the intricately carved ring in his hand, he broke down.

He waited for what seemed like hours. He drank bad coffee from the machine. He phoned his dad and told him briefly about Beth's operation. He didn't care what they thought about the pregnancy.

Beth would be fine, he kept telling himself. This was nothing like what happened to Caitlin and Madog. This was totally different. Fate couldn't be that cruel, surely? He broke down again. He couldn't lose her too. She was the love of his life.

Oh God! Why hadn't he told her that?

Finally, a nurse came in to see him.

Beth was out of surgery and was recovering in a side-ward.

She was still coming round when he entered the room. Her face was ashen and she looked exhausted. But she was here. She was with him.

He gently held her close to him and then sat beside her, holding her hand as she came out of the anaesthetic.

The doctor who'd performed the scan appeared, now dressed in surgical scrubs.

"Hi, Beth. Still a bit groggy?"

Beth murmured that she was okay.

"Well, we did the procedure. Removed the coil and performed the keyhole laparoscopy. We successfully cleared the ectopic tissue but the fallopian tube was ruptured, I'm afraid, and we had to take that too."

A sob escaped.

The doctor sat on the bed by her and touched her shoulder.

"Hey, you still have one healthy tube. You need time to heal. There are no guarantees, but plenty of women have babies with one tube, Beth."

Beth sniffed, trying to hold back the tears.

"Thank you, doctor."

As the door closed behind the doctor Beth sobbed again. And Gareth, holding onto her tightly, cried too.

CHAPTER 28

----------✳----------

The nurse came in and tactfully told Gareth it was time for him to go so Beth could rest.

She watched him through the side-ward window, shuffling down the corridor. His head was down. He was devastated. As long as he stayed with her, he'd never be a dad.

Her bag was at the end of the bed. It was sore to move, but she reached for it and checked her phone.

There were five missed video calls from Ellen. Gareth must have told them about the surgery.

Telling them she was pregnant; that must have been super-awkward for him. Then she remembered Caitlin. All the calls Ellen had made, they must be worried sick about her too.

She was sore, groggy and emotional, but it was better to get it over with now. Speak to Ellen and then get some sleep.

It was ironic, in the hospital she'd been Gareth's wife. They'd cried together after the doctor left. But he still hadn't managed to tell her he loved her.

Beth pressed the video call and Ellen came on the screen.

She was concerned. How was she feeling? Had she had something for the pain? She'd come and see her tomorrow, she said.

Beth felt overwhelmed as Ellen powered on.

"You'll be right as rain soon, Beth. Back to normal in no time."

"Ellen, they took the fallopian tube out."

Ellen grew quiet for a moment. The first time since they'd

started the call.

"I'm so sorry, dear. You poor thing. And Gareth too. He'll be gutted. He's always wanted a family. Of course, after he married the right woman. He's so good with Jake too."

It was what Beth had feared hearing the most.

She didn't take much in after that. Ellen rattled on and her mind drifted. In the end, she feigned tiredness and ended the call.

Her eyes flooded.

Gareth hadn't told his parents they were married. It was probably for the best.

And what had Ellen meant by 'the right woman'? Was she referring to Chantelle? Or was she telling her to leave so Gareth could find someone who could give him the family he wanted?

She'd seen Gareth with Jake. Ellen was right. He would be an amazing dad.

The doctor said they still had a chance.

She stared absently at the window out to the corridor. She meant the world to him, he'd said.

Was that enough?

The agreement. Friendship. Attraction. The sex. All that was simple. It was all the messy feelings around them that made everything so damn hard.

And now she had to end it.

She had to set him free.

The doctor grudgingly discharged her the next morning and Beth Morgan reluctantly left in a taxi to the station.

Gareth hadn't been able to get hold of Beth.

And when he arrived for visiting hours after lunch an elderly lady was sitting up in Beth's bed.

He scanned the ward. There was no sign of her. He hoped she'd not had a relapse.

With a churning gut, he approached the nurses' station.

"Can you tell me where Beth Morgan is, please?"

A nurse checked the patient records.

"She was discharged two hours ago. Said she was going home. We advised another night, but she said she was much better and the doctor agreed she could go."

He checked his phone. There were no messages.

He tried ringing her again, then again. It switched to voicemail each time. He left another message and sent a text.

'Beth, where are you?'

Maybe, she'd taken a taxi and gone back to the boathouse?

He drove home with the dreadful feeling growing in the pit of his stomach that she'd not be there.

Beth was gone.

And he'd never got to tell her how much he loved her.

Alys took one look at Beth standing at her front door and scooped her up into a huge hug, then put her in bed. Her friend was deathly pale. It was clear that she was exhausted.

Beth was in a state, but now was not the time to probe. Jo had told Alys all about the situation. It sounded complicated. What Beth needed was rest and time to clear her head.

She called Marcel and spent the next three days helping her friend slowly recover.

She was crying a lot. Hormones she said, but Alys didn't buy it. This wasn't just about the operation. Beth's heart was broken too.

At the weekend Jo called around. And with Beth feeling a little better, the three of them headed to a nearby bistro for lunch.

Alys gave Jo a look. They were both shocked at the change in Beth. She was flat. Depressed and lethargic.

Jo tried to snap her out of it.

"Beth? Have you heard a word we said?"

"Why don't you call Gareth?" Alys suggested. "He must be going out of his mind."

Beth stared at the bowl of pasta in front of her. Her appetite was completely gone.

"It's for the best."

"D'you still love him, Beth?"

Typical Jo, Alys thought. Cut to the chase, why don't you?

The agony in Beth's eyes confirmed it.

"Gareth was the love of my life. Perhaps I was his too. He never said. I dunno, maybe I was deluded, like with Jean-Paul. Anyway, it's over. He needs to move on and find someone who can give him the family he wants."

Jo butted in.

"Has he said that?"

"No, but his mother... "

"Never mind that old bag. Beth, you're not being fair. You've married him off, given him a couple of kids and probably a bloody labradoodle too, before you've even spoken to the poor chap. Seriously. Call him."

Alys gave Jo a hard stare.

Beth sniffed and Alys handed her a serviette.

"You can stay at mine for as long as you want. Marcel needs help. You can do a shift or two when you're feeling up to it. Get back into the cooking, it'll make you feel better."

Jo left Alys and Beth by the tube station.

She'd been gutted to see Beth like this. Whenever they'd spoken online, she'd had a glow about her. She'd been so happy. And she'd defended him to the hilt when Jo had grilled her. She'd been certain that this guy was 'the one', even if the both of them hadn't quite worked out all the details.

And, all this baloney about Gareth not telling her he loved her. She'd not told him, either.

They were as bad as each other. They'd been playing a huge

game of emotional chicken. Who'd blink first.

Well, she was a journalist. She was sure she could sort this. And besides, she felt sorry for this Gareth. Beth had disappeared out of his life without any explanation. That wasn't fair. Someone had to help him.

Walking through the London streets, she mulled over what she could and couldn't do.

She had Gareth's number.

Under the circumstances, there was no way she could butt in. Phone him up and get him rushing over to London straightaway.

Beth wasn't thinking rationally. If he charged in to whisk her back to Wales and it all went tits-up, then it might end things between them forever.

No, she needed a pretext. Something she could contact Gareth about. Where she could check the lie of the land, explain how Beth was with them, but wanted some time out to get over her loss.

And she'd have a word with him too while she was on the line about this 'love' business. Seriously? This dude needed to get his act together, and tell Beth what she needed to hear.

Jo had all the information about the planning objections. If she could get Gareth's project back on track, they'd both have the one thing that had brought them together. Evan's inheritance. Their dream.

CHAPTER 29

It had been a week and Beth still hadn't contacted Gareth, or come back to Freshwater Bay. When he called her number, it no longer connected. It was like it'd all been a dream and he'd woken up.

All her stuff was still in his house and he had no intention of moving it. The restaurant was ready to go, but again it stood empty. Alongside her old car. A solitary vehicle in the car park.

Gareth was a mess. He spent the first few days sitting in the boathouse brooding, rolling her wedding ring in the palm of his hand, drinking until the pain was numbed and he'd knocked himself out.

He couldn't eat. He couldn't think. All he felt was the darkest despair.

A blackness.

He'd lost the one thing he loved more than anything else. He would never love anyone like her again.

He needed Beth.

They'd been so good together. And now she was gone and he had no way of finding her.

And the baby. He ached when he thought about how much he would have loved being a dad.

It didn't matter if Beth couldn't have kids, they could foster or adopt. There were options and fertility treatments they could try.

It didn't matter if she didn't want that. As long as he was with her, together shoulder to shoulder through life. It was all that mattered.

Why hadn't he had the balls to admit to her or to himself how much he loved her?

He'd been a deluded coward who'd been too scared to handle his feelings.

His drawings were strewn across the kitchen peninsula. He ripped them up and threw them across the floor. The project was screwed. And without her, it was all a ridiculous pipe-dream, anyway. He'd never do it.

He had no idea where she was.

He didn't know her friends.

The truth was he didn't know much about Beth at all. Just that she'd worked in a French restaurant in London.

Jo had been up all night. It felt great. She was doing proper in-vestigative journalism again. Plus, she had a frontpage story.

The article was ready. It had all the sources listed underneath, as well as the evidence of undue influence. She'd called her con-tacts in the Cardiff newsroom and sent them the story.

They were chomping at the bit when they called back. They had to fly it by legals but the story was a runner. They could start with articles online and in the local papers straight away.

Taking Jo's line of enquiry, they'd got a local journalist digging into a similar development down the coast. If they could find the same pressures on planning applications as there were in Freshwater Bay, they'd expose a corruption story that could run and run.

Jo had found that Penfroz Holdings was one tiny thread of a much bigger corporation called PZH. And PZH had a serious bad-boy rep.

They specialised in buying up properties. Houses, pubs and land in prime undeveloped locations. They wheedled their way into a place and bought influence. And then, when they held all

THE STRICTLY BUSINESS PROPOSAL

the cards, they built their multi-million pound resorts.

These resorts that would never ordinarily pass planning consent. But, by the time PZH were finished, there were few locals left who hadn't been bought out or sold out. There was no one left to object.

That was what the letter to buy the restaurant had been about.

And to top it all, one of the directors listed under PZH was one Charles Fawksley-Brown. The same dude Beth had spoken to at the consultation meeting.

Buying property wasn't illegal. But undue influencing was.

She'd also called an entomology expert at a leading university. He confirmed that he'd be extremely interested in any rare moths, and agreed to help. It would be highly unusual, he said, to find rare breeds in such a windswept clifftop location.

Jo closed her laptop and reached for her mobile. What she was about to do broke all her girl codes.

He'd been an idiot. But Beth had been just as stupid; though she was too proud to admit it.

The whole baby thing was tricky. But, she was sure that if she could get them talking...

It was a huge risk. What she was about to do might cost her one of her best friends?

She weighed it up. Beth was definitely in love with him, and the chance of seeing her friend happy again was worth the flack she'd get for doing this.

She tapped in the number Beth had given her.

"Gareth?"

"Yes."

"It's Jo, Beth's friend... Yeah, yeah, she's fine. Well, she's better physically. She's still very upset and confused."

She rubbed her face as she listened to him on the other end of the line.

It was worse than she feared. The bloke was in a state. His voice was slurring and he was drunk.

He begged her to tell him where she was.

Then, he got upset.

Was he crying?

He loved her, he told her. He couldn't live without her.

It was all pouring out now.

Far too bloody late.

She interrupted him.

"You're telling the wrong one, pal. I can help you. Send me your email address. But you've got to get your shit together. You'll never get her back like this. There's some news about to hit the press. I think it'll kickstart your project. I'll call you back when I have more info, and when you've sobered up."

Madog was concerned. It had been a couple of weeks now and Gareth still wasn't coping. He wasn't speaking to any of the family and he'd been holed up in the boathouse.

If anyone knew about loss, it was him. He'd been grieving for months now and at the start, he'd been in a dark place too. If it hadn't been for Jake...

He shook his head.

The pain had gotten easier to bear, but there was no denying that losing Caitlin had blown a massive hole in his life, and his heart.

With the milking done, he turned the cows back into the field. Back at the farmhouse his mother always had a plate of bacon and eggs ready for him for when he'd finished the morning shift.

"Can you look after Jake this afternoon," he asked her as he sat down to eat.

Ellen nodded. She'd already got Jake up and had fed him while Madog was milking.

"I'm going to see Gareth. See if I can talk some sense into him."

Ellen set a mug of tea down for her son.

"Is that wise, love? You know how he gets. He broods. He needs a little time and then he'll get over it. Like he did the last one."

Madog stared at his mother hard. She'd not liked Beth since she'd shown her up with that pie.

"The last one? Open your eyes, Mam. Beth is no Chantelle."
Ellen sat down.

"But she's a city girl. She'll never make him happy."
Madog put his knife and fork down.

"Mam, I've never seen Gareth like this before. He's crazy about her. She is about him too, I'm sure of it. It's the real deal."
She studied her hands.

"I might have said something."

"What did you do?"
Ellen sniffed.

"I might have said something to Beth. Said how Gareth always wanted to be a father."

"What?"

"I was upset. He's always so private. Then this pregnancy business. He'd lied to us. It was like he pushed us out of his life. I was only trying to do the best for him."

"Mam!"

"I'm sorry, love. Let me try and fix it."

"No, " Madog warned her. "Stay out of it. I'll talk to him."

Madog was shocked at the state of Gareth when he opened the door.

His face was drawn. He'd not shaved for days. And by the looks of it, he'd been wearing the same dirty T-shirt.

He was sober though; that was progress.

Gareth moved out of the door frame and Madog went in.

It still stank like a brewery in there.

Bottles of beer and whisky cluttered the worktops, alongside unwashed plates with half-chewed food still on them.

"Mate! What's been going on?"

His face was dazed.

He shook his head.

Madog held out his arms. It was all he could do.

Gareth buried his head on his youngest brother's shoulder and broke down.

"She's gone. And she's not coming back."

Madog held him as Gareth cried.

He let him get it out of his system. It was the only way. He was so much younger than his brother, but the recent months had made him grow up fast.

Gareth pulled away, trying to regain control.

"I'm sorry, Madog."

"S'alright... I'm gonna make you a coffee. And then you're gonna get cleaned up."

Madog was gathering all the empty bottles into a bin bag when Gareth's phone went off.

He could hear the shower going upstairs, so he decided he'd better answer it. Take a message.

"Gareth?"

"Uhh... I'm actually his... "

Madog frowned as the female voice abruptly cut across him.

"Yeah, yeah, I'm super-busy too. This won't take long. I've talked it through with Alys who Beth's staying with. We're not going to tell you where she is. If Beth wants to get in touch, she will."

Madog cleared his throat.

"*Uhh*... Is she coming back?"

"Can't call it. She loves you, Gareth. God knows why. You've been a complete prat."

Madog smirked.

"Alys has got Beth doing some shifts back in La Vie. It's a start but she's still all over the place. I'll try talking to her again, but it might take a while. She's still gutted about the op. She's worried she can't have kids and you won't want her."

Madog struggled with what to say about that. He looked up the stairs. Gareth still wasn't about.

"No, she's wrong. We need to talk it through."

It was the best he could come up with.

"Funny, that's what I said too."

Madog rubbed his chin, unsure of what to say next.

"Umm... Tell her I love her, will you?"

"You're joking me, right?"

She ended the call leaving Madog none the wiser and deeply regretting answering Gareth's phone.

Madog was finishing up by the time Gareth came back downstairs showered and shaved. The dishwasher was going and there was a bin bag of bottles in the back of his Land Rover.

"Feeling better?"

Gareth gave him the ghost of a smile as he made them another coffee. His face was still gaunt. He'd lost a lot of weight.

"You know," Madog began. "Caitlin's gone forever and I can't change that. But Beth's still alive. There's always a chance. And I've just taken a call for you. From her friend."

"Jo?"

"Was that her name? She was a bit of a madam. She thought I was you. I got a flea in my ear."

Madog smirked.

"Apparently, you're a prat. And you need to tell Beth you love her."

He studied his brother's face.

"What? You didn't do that? Jo's right. You are a prat. What's wrong with you?"

Gareth shrugged.

"It was complicated."

"And now isn't? She still loves you, bro. But she's worried you're not going to want her if you can't be a dad."

"She said that?"

"They wouldn't tell me where she was. But she's working in the restaurant again. La Vie something?"

"En Rose... La Vie en Rose. Evan went there every Friday at two."

Gareth grabbed his laptop.

"What you doing?"

"Booking a train ticket."

Madog laughed and flicked his brother's ear.

"About bloody time! By the way, I've got myself a date tomorrow night. With Anwen. I owe you one."

Gareth played with Evan's ring as he waited for the train information page to load. He'd put it back onto his left ring finger.

He was a married man and he didn't care who knew it. He was a married man who needed to see his wife.

CHAPTER 30

----------*---------

I t was a quiet Friday afternoon in La Vie en Rose and Beth was cooking sea bass under the salamander grill.

It required intense concentration. Thirty seconds under and the flesh near the bones would be translucent and underdone; thirty seconds over and the whole thing would turn dry.

Marcel had noticed the change in her at once. Was it that obvious? When Alys had asked, he'd instantly given her some shifts. But after the first shift, he'd stuck her on the fish where she could focus on the dishes.

He was right. She was still hurting.

Alys had been great. She'd researched fertility problems and helped reassure her that the odds weren't that bad. Even so, the chance that she might never have a baby made Beth sad.

Jo had been more difficult. She kept defending Gareth, telling her to talk to him. That wasn't what Beth wanted to hear. She'd come to London for a safe space, not to be nagged at.

She'd got a new sim card and phoned all her suppliers and potential staff. She cancelled everything and paid her bills. Alys had helped her with clothes and things until she got sorted. Everything was still in Freshwater Bay. But she'd closed the door on that life now.

It was two o'clock, Friday afternoon and Gareth sat down at table twelve in La Vie En Rose. He was antsy and he'd hardly slept for thinking about this moment.

The waiter tried to hand him a menu but Gareth held up his hand.

"Is it possible to have something made to order?"

"Uhh..."

The waiter's eyes flicked around the restaurant searching in vain for his manager.

"Uhh... I'll have to ask the chefs."

"Is Beth working?"

He felt the butterflies in his stomach.

"Yes, she is."

"Can you ask her if table twelve can have scallops on pea purée with cockles and a laverbread tuile, please? Did you get that?"

The waiter wrote it on his pad

"Scallops, peas, cockles... *laverbread tuile*?... Sir, I'm not sure we have..."

"Just ask her."

The waiter finished writing and disappeared behind the stainless steel door.

Gareth fixed his eyes on it.

His gut twisted. Even if he left here alone, he had to tell her he loved her.

"Order from table twelve. They want something off-menu. Can you do it, Beth?"

"Depends. What is it?"

"Scallops on pea purée with cockles and a laverbread tuile."

She felt the blood draining from her. Her legs were suddenly weak and she steadied herself with her hand on the stainless-steel workbench.

"Tell them.... Tell them... No."

The waiter came back a couple of minutes later.

"Can you do a crab with grapefruit salad, then?"

What was he doing to her? Her throat was dry and her pulse was racing. Should she go through and see him?

She hadn't been prepared for this. She didn't think he'd come. She stalled for time.

"Tell him, I'll see what I can do."

What was she going to do? She couldn't think straight.

He'd come to see her, but there was no way she could go back to him if it didn't mean anything, apart from sex. She couldn't live like that. It only meant anything if it was love. If he told her that he loved her.

Her stomach knotted.

If she raced out there and told him that she loved him, she'd only have her heart broken, again.

She made the salad and sent it out.

Gareth was running out of ideas.

He played with the ring on his finger as he thought about his next move.

When she'd said she couldn't do the scallops and didn't come out of the kitchen, he'd nearly got up and left. It was a slap in the face.

He'd waited twenty minutes and there was still no sign of Beth. He'd wait at that table all day and night if he had to.

He could go into the kitchen anyway. Go in and find her?

He rejected that idea. He'd wind up getting arrested for stalking her.

No. If she wanted to see him, she'd come out. He'd made it plain enough that he was here.

Then, the salad arrived.

It was just as beautiful as he remembered.

No one else could do a salad like that. And she'd made it for him.

Savouring the taste in his mouth as he took a bite from his

fork, he cast his mind back grimly to her lesson on the senses. The memory tortured him as he remembered how happy they'd been.

He'd expected her to bring the salad out to him, but it came with the waiter. Was that a sign that she wanted him to go away?

He tried, but he couldn't swallow another mouthful of the food.

He pushed the plate away.

Had this been a mistake? Where was she?

He felt sick with the bitter gall of truth.

She wasn't coming.

It was over.

The waiter came to the table to take his plate.

"Is everything alright with your food, Sir?"

"Yes. Can you give this to the chef, please? Tell her it's from her husband."

The waiter came back into the kitchen carrying a barely touched plate of crab and grapefruit salad.

In his other hand was a small velvet pouch.

The waiter handed it to Beth.

"He said it was for you."

She glanced at the uneaten salad, then shakily opened the pouch. Gareth had rejected her food because he'd come to give her back her ring.

To let her go.

The waiter went back out. At table twelve a banknote now lay on the tablecloth where Gareth had sat.

"Beth, mate. Sorry, I forgot to tell you. The velvet pouch. The guy said he was your husband. He was definitely married. He had a ring on his left-hand finger. Been keeping that one quiet, Chef."

Beth crashed out of the kitchen into the restaurant in her fish stained whites.

She fixed her eyes on table twelve. It was empty.

Heads turned as she rushed through the tables and out the door onto the busy London street.

She desperately searched through the crowds.

But he wasn't there.

He'd given up and gone.

Slumping down by a shop front, she drew her head up to her knees and wept.

CHAPTER 31

----------✳---------

Gareth first noticed that there was someone new in the restaurant when he'd seen the vans in the car park earlier on that week. Last night there'd been a light on in the apartment too.

He wasn't sure what was going on. She'd probably leased the place out. It'd make good business sense.

He'd go there one day. But not now.

His pickup passed the restaurant in the dark as Gareth headed for the early train and the five-hour journey to London.

He'd not heard from Beth, or from Jo.

But encouraged again by Madog, he wasn't giving up. Beth was his wife. Even if it had been about business initially, they'd made solemn vows together. Vows that couldn't be broken easily. And with his hand on his heart, he could say that when they'd stood together on that day they'd both known that it would mean more.

Their love had been as inevitable as the dawn after the dark. And he'd never stop loving her.

But neither could he face being here.

Freshwater Bay reminded him too much of their past together. When he looked up at the restaurant, he saw her anxious face as she'd placed those dishes in front of him, eager for him to taste. When he gazed out at the islands, all he could see was their night on the boat.

It was torture.

He needed to be with her in the present, not the past.

He had to try and get in touch with her again. He knew where she worked and he wouldn't give up.

His plan was to move to London.

Hell, he'd become Evan Morgan. Mr Friday Two O'clock Table. Whatever it took to get her back.

He had an interview. It was a prestigious multinational firm and it would be a step up in his career if he got it.

He didn't care about that. Only about Beth.

He was feeling excited and positive again. He'd go to La Vie straight after he arrived, see if he could catch her at the restaurant and share his plans.

She had the ring and that gave him hope.

The long train journey was more arduous than ever. He struggled to concentrate on the book he'd bought and couldn't focus on reviewing his presentation.

He was as jittery as hell. He'd made the mistake of not waiting around for Beth at the restaurant the last time. He had to be more resilient. He'd only give up this time once he got to tell her he loved her.

If she told him that she didn't love him, then he'd stop. But he didn't want to think about that right now.

At Paddington Station's entrance, he saw a young student embrace his girlfriend as she got off the train.

He turned away. Was he always to be reminded of her?

The afternoon was warm, and La Vie's lunchtime service was in full swing when he arrived at the front entrance.

He queued up at the door, trying to look inside. Two customers in front of him were fussing with their coats and complaining about their table. They wanted one by the window not by the toilets.

Gareth waited impatiently as a smartly dressed man placated them. He couldn't wait around like this. He needed to see her.

"Sir?"

A voice snapped Gareth from his distracted thoughts.

"Sir, do you have a table booked with us this afternoon?"
Gareth noticed the French accent.
"Are you Marcel, Beth's boss?"
He stared at Gareth, like he was sizing him up.
"I need to see her urgently. Is she here?"
"No monsieur."
This wasn't how it was meant to go.
"No. No. She has to be, you don't understand." he said feeling panic welling up within.
"I tell you, she's not."
"Are you sure? I've got a job interview at four. I'm moving here. I need Beth in my life."
Marcel shifted uncomfortably as one or two tables near them turned their way.
"Sir. Please, the other customers."
"I need to tell her I love her, at least. Please can you help me?
Gareth stared at him, his eyes pleading.
"You're Gareth right?"
Marcel came around the counter to him, guiding him towards the door.
"She's gone," he said quietly.
"Where?"
"Back to Wales."
Marcel winked at him as they went out onto the busy street.
"She said she was going home to run her restaurant."
Gareth felt his heart pounding as he shook Marcel's hand vigorously.
"Thank you."
He checked his phone. The last train was at five o'clock. If he rushed, he'd make it.
Gareth Morgan was going home too.

Beth Morgan stepped out of the busy kitchen for a five-minute break. She stood on the deck of La Galloise restaurant and looked out to the islands across the bay.

She'd changed the restaurant's name slightly. She owned it, after all. And no one, not even Gareth Morgan was going to stop her from achieving her dream.

She thought back to the wreck she was a couple of weeks ago. After Gareth left La Vie, Marcel had called Alys, and Jo had turned up too to take her home.

Then, they'd talked and talked.

And it hadn't been easy listening. They'd given her some bitter truths. Made her realise what a fool she'd been. If he'd hurt her before, she'd broken Gareth too. She'd been cruel to him. Caused him pain.

The feelings she had for him were too powerful. She'd been trying to protect her heart. She'd been too scared to leave the kitchen and face him.

And it was Jo who'd listened and convinced her that Beth Morgan was not the simpering, lovesick fool she was at nineteen.

She was twenty-nine years old, a strong independent woman who needed to do something more with her life. And Evan Morgan had given her a precious gift.

She'd eaten humble pie and the suppliers and staff were back on board. It had only been a month's delay, and when she'd called them most of her staff had picked up summer work which was now coming to an end.

Jo was coming up in October and was going to do a piece on the restaurant for her online newsfeed. She needed all the publicity she could get to help drum up customers through the winter months.

She was going to tough this one out. Until he divorced her, Beth would be Mrs Morgan and she'd wear his ring on her left hand. She wasn't embarrassed to show him that she still loved him and she wasn't going to hide the fact that she was a married woman.

Even if he had another woman in his life by now, she'd deal with it with her head held high. Even when he got remarried to someone else. Even when he had children.

She was determined she could live with that, even though it meant not being able to have him again.

It felt right to be in Freshwater Bay. This was where she belonged, even if she was alone.

The first night's service in La Galloise had gone as well as Beth could have hoped for. It had been bookings only, a trial run.

The customers were all very positive. Only when she saw the online reviews would she know for sure what the real feedback was.

There was a hiccup with one of the younger chefs who was running late on his dishes. He'd been nervous, but he had potential and was as keen as mustard. She enjoyed training the juniors. She'd been there once herself.

The cocktail bar was proving a big hit and a group of friends on the deck were finishing off their drinks. She'd called time but they were in no hurry to leave. The September air was warm and it was still pleasant outside. If she was lucky they'd have an Indian summer.

Marcel called her before the shift. Gareth had been to the restaurant again. They'd talked briefly and Gareth told him he was going for a job interview.

After she'd reflected on the news, she decided he probably wanted to discuss the divorce. The lights of the boathouse were off and the place was deserted. He'd left Freshwater Bay.

She shook herself; enough of feeling sad.

Returning to the kitchen, she made sure the staff were cleaning down properly at the end of the shift. It was important to establish good habits from the get-go.

Lifting a pile of clean plates from the back, she took them through to the shelving in the front storage area.

The heavy restaurant doors rattled as they opened.

It was well after eleven and she wasn't about to serve any more drinkers.

"Sorry, the bar's closed," she called out as she kneeled under the serving area, stacking the plates tidily away.

"Beth."

Her heart thumped.

But he was in London?

Straightening up, she stared apprehensively at the man walking towards her through the restaurant.

She was shocked. He was the shadow of the man he was. His slightly crumpled oversized navy suit and the familiar cornflower blue shirt now loose at the collar. His face was pale. And there was a sadness about him.

"Gareth."

They stood a few feet apart from each other, like gunfighters in a saloon, across the restaurant floor.

Who was going to make the first move?

She held firm, unsure of what to do next.

She was desperate to embrace him but she could see he was trying to get his words together. Probably about the divorce.

She composed herself. Stay tough, cold like ice.

He was pointing to her hand.

"The ring. It's on your left finger."

She nodded, then gasped.

"Yours is too."

He edged towards her.

She'd fixed her face, but her heart was betraying her, pumping hard.

"Beth, you're the love of my life and I was a fool for not telling you that."

He walked towards her, to embrace her.

But she stepped back.

"I hear you're moving to London."

"I hear you're back. I like the view much better here."

Was he talking about her?

"Beth, I love you and I can't live without you."

She went to him then, reaching up and touching his sunken cheek.

His eyes gazed searchingly into hers as he placed his arms around her and held her close.

Overwhelmed with emotion, she rested her head on his chest,

hearing his heart beating underneath his shirt.

"I should never have left you. I'm sorry that I caused you so much pain," she uttered into his chest. "I went after you, that day in the restaurant, but you'd already gone."

"You did?"

"Yes. I love you so much it hurts."

He gently lifted her chin and found her lips."

She pulled away.

She had to be sure.

"What if we can't have children?"

"I'll take whatever we're given, Beth. It's *you* I want in my life. Beside me forever."

That was enough for her.

She melted into his arms as they kissed.

As they drew apart, he took both of her hands in his.

"I want to change the terms of our agreement."

He bent down on one knee.

"Beth Morgan, I want everyone to know we're married. Will you be beside me forever as my wife?"

Overwrought, she joined him on the floor.

"Yes. Gareth, will you be my husband?"

"Yes, cariad. Right here, right now and happily ever after."

Her face cracked into a broad smile.

They kissed until Beth remembered that there were still staff in the kitchen and customers on the deck.

"I've missed you so much, Beth."

Looking deep into his eyes, she raked back his hair.

"Me too. But look at you? I need to feed you up. You've gone so skinny."

He smiled and brushed her lightly on the lips.

"I can't live without you, Mrs Morgan."

They lay in bed in the boathouse wrapped in each other's arms. The dawn was breaking and they needed to sleep.

"We did do things a bit backwards didn't we?" Gareth said, thinking aloud.

"Hmm."

"I hope you're not too upset that you didn't get the big dress and the ten bridesmaids. We can do it again, if you like?"

"What? Have another wedding?"

"If you want."

Beth considered it for a minute.

"Gareth Morgan, I had the most perfect wedding day. No more weddings, please."

"Suits me."

They lay in contented silence for a moment, Beth's head resting on his chest. His heart was full.

"Well then, how about another tango? Buenos Aires; for our honeymoon?"

Beth tilted her head up towards his.

"Perfect."

Gareth squeezed Beth's hand as they nervously entered the kitchen of Cae Môr Farm that afternoon. There was no more putting it off.

David looked up from his newspaper and Ellen wiped her hands as she turned from the sink to see who'd walked in.

Gareth wove his fingers tightly into Beth's.

"Mam, Dad... meet my wife."

Ellen sat down beside David, speechless.

They listened to Gareth as he told them the whole story. He explained Evan's will and the business proposal, and how they'd fallen in love.

David leaned back in his chair.

"Well, that's my brother for you. A wily old fox. And an excellent judge of character."

He got up and went over to Beth and gave her a warm embrace.

"Welcome to the family."

Ellen, who'd been watching her son intently, did the same.

"I'm so pleased for you both."

Ellen held on to her for a moment longer.

"I'm sorry," she whispered quietly into her ear.

Beth nodded to her as they pulled apart. She'd not toldGareth about the call.

"I've now got a daughter."

Beth took a deep breath.

"Yes, you have."

EPILOGUE

----------✳︎---------

I t's time, she told herself as she rolled down her pants. She'd been putting it off, desperate not to be disappointed again. A few months before, the one miserable line had quickly snuffed out all hope. But, this time she'd missed three periods.

She held the stick into the flow of urine with nervous anticipation. Were their lives about to change, or not?

It was one of those moments. Like when the black-rimmed card came through the post about Evan's passing, or when the proposal text came through from Gareth.

The time had passed quickly. After Jo exposed the dodgy deals and the press had a field day, planning permission had been swiftly granted. Gareth had now nearly completed his development.

There were three local families in the eco-chalets, and the bookings for the holiday chalets were strong. They were boosted also by five letting rooms which Gareth had remodelled in the apartment above the restaurant.

Gareth's designs had won a regional award and he was doing more consultancy these days, working from the spare room in the boathouse.

The restaurant was crazy busy. Her deputy Head Chef, Paul was leading the shift tonight. It was Tuesday and there were forty booked in. She never imagined that it would take off like this.

She'd also had some rave reviews, and last weekend her restaurant appeared in a national Sunday newspaper in a list of top places to eat by the seaside.

It was important to keep balance in their lives. Beth was trying, although it didn't come naturally to her, and she'd work fifteen-hour days if she could. She'd tried her best not to recently; she didn't want to take any risks this time around.

Gareth had suggested that they shut each year for the whole of January. It was an inspired idea. They'd travelled to South America where, as promised, they tangoed in Buenos Aires and then headed north to see the waterfalls of Iguazu and the beaches of Brazil.

She came home with a head full of recipes. From meaty Argentinian asados to Brazilian street food. Crispy and creamy Brazilian cod balls had gone straight on the menu and were now a top seller.

She packed the test back in the box and slipped it into her back trouser pocket.

Penfroz had approached her two weeks ago about leasing the Lobster Pot. After the scandal they were restructuring.

It was an opportunity and a risk. She would only do it if she had someone she could trust on board. She'd love that person to be Alys. But Alys had secured herself a job in the best patisserie in Paris and was messaging Beth daily with her mind-blowing desserts. She wasn't coming to Freshwater Bay any time soon.

Beth came into the living area of the boathouse and sat down beside Gareth on the sofa, snuggling up to him as he put his arm around her.

The nights were just starting to cool off and they sat inside, looking out at the sea.

"This is so nice."

Gareth felt a hard lump with corners in the back of her trousers. "What've you got there?"

She sat up, looking at him coyly.

"Nothing."

"Liar. In the back of your jeans. What've you got?"

He tickled her.

"Alright, alright," she laughed.

She reached into her back pocket.

"It's for you. Open it."

He stared at the stick inside.

"Two lines. That means?...oh my God... Are you? Are we going to...?"

"Yes, we are. I'm not sure when. I've missed a couple of periods. I've been too scared to check 'til now. I'll have to see the doctor and get a scan."

"Yesss!"

He hugged her tight, then kissed her.

"I'm going to be a dad. Wow! Let me see."

She lay flat on the sofa, laughing as he lifted her top, unbuttoned her jeans and gently ran his hand over her.

"Can you feel a bump yet?"

His face beamed at her.

"Yes, I can. A little one."

"Beth?"

"Hmm?"

"I was thinking, the name?"

Beth smacked him with the cushion.

"Tell your mother, our baby will *not* be called Puffin."

He kissed her belly, making her giggle.

"Then, how about Finn?"

Beth considered it for a moment or two.

"Yes, I like that. Boy or a girl, Finn it is."

Gareth sealed his proposal with a kiss.

"Finn. Our little adventuresome kayaker."

ABOUT BOOK TWO

The Freshwater Bay Series continues in:
The Actor's Deceit - Ariana and Rhys

How dare he?

He said he hated it here. So why come back and upset her world, just when Ariana Jones is starting to make a name for herself as a serious jewellery designer? Just when she's met someone else.

Actor Rhys Morgan needs to make big changes to his life and fast. That means leaving Tinsel Town and going back home to Wales. But home's not been his happy place.

He's told too many people too many lies. What will they say when they find out that this Hollywood star was really working in an L.A. bar?

And what will Ariana Jones, the woman who hates him the most say when he tells her he still loves her?

The lies are killing him, but the truth will break them.

PRAISE FOR AUTHOR

What Amazon and Goodreads readers are saying:

★ ★ ★ ★ ★ *"This book kept me wanting more. A cracking read. Can't wait for the next one."*

★ ★ ★ ★ ★ *"Great characters, beautiful depictions of West Wales, confusion and misunderstandings create a great read. This is a terrific love story."*

★ ★ ★ ★ ★ *"What a great story! Loved all of the people in it, as they were believable. I could see the sights and places as well as the people in my mind's eye. Would love to read more stories by Nell Grey."*

★ ★ ★ ★ ★ *"Really enjoyed this love story between Beth and Gareth. Totally captivating and struggled to put it down. Really looking forward to book 2."*

Printed in Great Britain
by Amazon

53569478R00139